JUDE

Servant Siblings Series: Book 4

JENIFER JENNINGS

For Liz, may God use your dedication to further His kingdom.

"And awe came upon every soul, and many wonders and signs were being done through the apostles."

-Acts 2:43

CHAPTER 1

Jude reached for the knob on the Ark of Scrolls with trembling fingers. The wooden cabinet containing copies of the recordings of Moses and the prophets loomed over him adding to the weight of the moment. The gathering of teachers in the modest synagogue rose behind him in silent unison sending a shiver up his back. He swallowed past the lump in his throat and pulled open the first door followed by the second.

As rows of scrolls stood exposed, the distinct scent of parchment flooded his senses. He longed to stand still and savor the moment. The sacred documents lay waiting for him as a woman beckoning her lover. His fingers ached to unroll each one and drink in the words of his ancestors.

Beads of sweat formed on his brow as he fought the urge to wipe them away. Meticulously, he looked to the top row and searched for the correct scroll. This was a rare opportunity and one which rested on how well he spoke before the prominent men Rabbi Ethan had invited to attend the day's reading.

When Ethan offered for Jude to read in his synagogue for the chance to be asked to sit at the feet of a Rabbi, Jude considered selecting a scroll from Ezekiel or Daniel. He knew such deep readings would provide thought-provoking meat for the religious leaders to chew. He wanted to show the world, or at least the men that filled the bench seating of Ethan's synagogue, that he would make a good Rabbi. After much prayer, and even more doubt, he instead chose a well-known story of Abba Abraham and hoped to provide fresh insight considering recent events. He concluded that there was no better way to win the hearts of the children of Abraham than to speak from one of his stories.

Selecting what he hoped was the right scroll, he held the parchment to his chest, turned, and took careful steps toward the Scroll Table. Dropping a sacred scroll would be devastating to his chances of becoming a student. In addition, Rabbi Ethan would never let him read in his synagogue again.

Laying the parchment on the flat stone table, Jude cautiously unrolled the scroll. To his delight, the familiar words of the story caught his eyes as he continued to open the sacred writings. Grabbing the wrong parchment would have certainly revealed his inexperience.

Once the scroll was opened enough across the table, Jude took a breath and, starting at the far right, read, "After these things Adonai tested Abraham and said to him, 'Abraham!' And he said, 'Here I am.' He said, 'Take your son, your only son Isaac, whom you love, and go to the land of Moriah, and offer him there as a burnt offering on one of the mountains of which I shall tell you.'

Jude glanced up for a moment as he watched several men nod in approval. He returned his gaze to the parchment and read, "So, Abraham rose early in the morning, saddled his donkey, and took two of his young men, and his son Isaac. He cut the wood for the burnt offering and went to the place Adonai had told him."

He paused as he heard shaking in his voice. With a steadying breath, he continued, "On the third day Abraham lifted his eyes and saw the place from afar. Then Abraham said to his young men, 'Stay here with the donkey; I and the boy will go over there and worship and we will come again to you.' Abraham took the wood of the burnt offering and laid it on Isaac. He took in his hand the fire and the knife.

"And Isaac said to his father Abraham, 'My father!' And he said, 'Here I am, my son.' He said, 'Behold, the fire and the wood, but where is the lamb for a burnt offering?' Abraham said, 'Adonai will provide for Himself the lamb for a burnt offering.'"

Jude battled within himself as he faltered over some of the ancient words. He'd practiced the reading as often as he could but he didn't have the skill in his ancestors' tongue as those who had continued to read it from their youth. Working as a craftsman had called for him to use the wider spoken Greek tongue in order to communicate with a more varied group of co-laborers. He knew even some of the most prominent men in the Temple read the Greek translation of the recordings but he was determined to read from Ethan's scrolls which had been copied in the language of their people.

He vied for the courage to look up and find Rabbi Ethan standing among the crowd. He wanted to see encouragement on the older man's face. Yet, he considered the possibility that disappointment might be discovered instead. With reluctance, he kept his eyes on the scroll of Moses allowing the words to provide the comfort he sought.

Jude lifted a silent plea for Adonai to strengthen his

voice as he continued to read, "When they came to the place of which Adonai had told him, Abraham built the altar there and laid the wood in order and bound Isaac and laid him on the altar. Then Abraham reached out and took the knife to slaughter his son. But the angel of Adonai called to him and said, 'Abraham, Abraham!' And he said, 'Here I am.' He said, 'Do not lay your hand on the boy for now I know that you fear Adonai, seeing as you have not withheld your son from me.'

"Abraham lifted his eyes and looked, and behind him was a ram caught in a thicket by his horns. Abraham went and took the ram and offered it up as a burnt offering instead of his son. So, Abraham called the name of the place, 'Adonai will provide' as it is said to this day, 'On the mount of Adonai it shall be provided.'"

With fingers still shaking, Jude rolled up the scroll, gently delivered the parchment back to its proper place in the holy cabinet, and closed the doors.

The gathering took their seats as Jude turned to face them once more. His mind swirled with everything he wanted to share. He feared opening his mouth would release a flood of muddled words and thoughts but he knew this was his opportunity to take a step closer to his dream. This would be the moment to show his potential as a student. A chance that might not resurface.

Jude elected not to sit, as was the custom, but paced

the bema determined to display confidence even as his innards quaked. "As Isaac was willingly led to the mount of Adonai, so too was Jesus, my brother, willingly led to a hill to die. Two men accompanied Abraham and Isaac as two thieves hung on either side of Jesus."

Finally finding the courage to search the faces, Jude found Rabbi Ethan's impartial gaze. The two had discussed the similarities between Isaac and Jesus at length in the days leading up to the reading. Jude hoped he could provide enough evidence for the men present to make the same connections he had through his studies.

"Abba Abraham placed the wood for the burnt offering on the back of Isaac. My brother carried the beam of his cross on his shoulders. Abraham told Isaac that Adonai would provide a lamb for the offering and a ram was provided whose horns were caught in a bush. As my brother hung naked and bleeding from his cross with a crown of thorns encircling his head, no other was found to take his place. Adonai provided. He is the lamb…" Jude paused as the words of his cousin, John, came forward, "Jesus is 'the Lamb of Adonai, who takes away the sin of the world.'"

CHAPTER 2

Murmurings from the men told Jude he had struck the place in their minds for which he was hoping.

An older man spoke first, "Are we to assume you are attempting to provide evidence that your brother is Messiah?"

"Assume what you will," Jude answered. "As I study the scrolls, I can come to no other conclusion."

"You've barely enough hair on your chin to count yourself a man," another sneered. "I doubt you've studied long enough to make any conclusions."

Jude brushed his thick beard as he felt the blow find its mark in his soul. He feared that very thing to be true as he met eyes with Rabbi Ethan.

The teacher merely dipped his head as a sign for Jude to continue with his lesson.

"It is true I have not been blessed to study the scrolls as long as some of you," Jude spoke slowly to not let embarrassment color his words, "but I walked beside my brother. I saw his character, and I've seen miracles performed."

"Tricks from a flattering tongue," someone cried out.

Jude searched for the source but couldn't place the voice among the collection of men.

"There have been many who've taken their last breath on a Roman cross," another added. "Why should we count your brother any different than those who have made similar claims and been discovered as blasphemers?"

Jude turned toward the man who posed the question. "How many of those men walked out of their graves days later?"

The room fell silent.

"Hear me," Jude pleaded. "My brother died as your substitute as the ram died for Isaac. He is Messiah."

The gathering erupted into heated conversations.

Jude's heart jumped into his throat. He knew his findings would be difficult for the men to believe; they had been difficult for him to believe at first. He hoped his words would be enough to sway them but his lack of experience had revealed itself. How did Jesus make teaching look so easy?

Heated shouts from red-faced men took Jude back to a day many years ago when Jesus spoke in the synagogue of Nazareth early in his ministry. His claim of fulfilling Isaiah's prophecy had driven the men wild enough to attempt to throw him from the cliff upon which their city had been built. Thankfully, Jesus had been able to escape their blood lust.

In exchange for his life, Jesus had lost the

opportunity to ever speak in his home synagogue again. Without proper training from a local Rabbi, Jesus continued his journey to becoming a teacher on his own. The blasphemy of his brother had marred Jude's reputation with the same stroke. He had not been taken seriously while his oldest brother continued to claim he was the one the Spirit of Adonai had anointed.

Jude envied Jesus. Not only was his oldest brother a craftsman of stone and wood but also of words. He could weave stories and parables that would leave people speechless. Words did not easily pour from Jude's lips. Today's reading confirmed that fear. His words sounded more like a babbling mudslide than a rich flowing river. Returning to work in a quarry was not what Jude wanted to do with the rest of his life. He wanted more than anything to be a Rabbi.

He was keenly aware of the fact that Rabbis don't make much money. Even as eloquent and popular as Jesus had become, he still went to his grave with no fortune to his name and spent the last three years of his life depending upon the financial support of prominent women. Jude's family had needed money more than another traveling Rabbi, and his local teachers had condemned him based on his older brother's absurd declarations of Messiahship. Resigning to his fate of being a meager craftsman for the rest of his life, Jude had reluctantly set his dream aside and focused his attention on the work of his hands.

With the recent trip to Jerusalem and the events of his brother's death, resurrection, and growing following, Jude reveled in his studies with Rabbi Ethan. Every moment he could be spared from working with James and the disciples was spent in Ethan's synagogue. When Jude shared his dream with the Rabbi, the older man graciously offered to invite local teachers to a reading in the hopes one would extend an invitation to Jude.

Jesus' steps to becoming a Rabbi had led him to a cross. As Jude looked around the room of men yelling over one another, he wondered if he continued to follow this path if it would lead to the same end.

With hands spread in front of him, Jude silently pleaded with Ethan to calm the chaos.

Rabbi Ethan rose and, with raised arms, cried out, "Enough."

The local teachers reluctantly settled, some of them shouting their last thoughts in the growing silence.

When the noise ceased, Ethan lowered his arms. "I did not invite you here today to battle this young man with the swords of your views. Jude has shown great potential as a student."

Jude's heart raced at the commendation.

"As many of you know, there are fewer and fewer who wish to dedicate themselves to a teacher; to the study of Torah." Ethan cast a heavy gaze around the room. "We do not want our history to be forgotten. How can we deny one so willing?"

The men shared agreeable mutterings among themselves.

Ethan moved toward the front, placing himself in front of Jude. "I think that is enough for today." He spoke a short prayer of thanks and dismissed the gathering.

With murmurs and whispered conversations, the men stood and filtered out of the synagogue.

Jude stepped off the bema toward the thinning crowd. His eyes caught the one person whose attention he most wished to capture. "Rabbi Gamaliel."

The older man halted and turned toward him.

Jude cleared the space between them with haste. "Rabbi, thank you for attending today's reading. I was hoping to speak with you…" His words dropped as he watched Saul come up behind the Rabbi. The younger man's face held a smirk, but Jude couldn't decipher if his poor reading was the cause of Saul's grin or if he always looked so arrogant. He returned his attention to Gamaliel who was waiting for him to continue. "I wanted to ask if you had room for another student."

The older Rabbi looked down at Jude's hands. "I think you are best suited to working with your hands," his scrutinizing eyes traveled upward to Jude's face, "and let others concern themselves with studying and teaching Torah."

Jude tucked his hands into the folds of his tunic and bowed his head. "I understand."

The highly respected teacher and his student left the synagogue together.

Jude pulled his hands from his tunic and studied them. Rough calluses covered his palms. Cuts that had healed, re-opened, and healed repeatedly by stone marred his olive skin. He rubbed at the scars and coarse skin as disdain grew in him. He should have been learning at the feet of a great Rabbi like Gamaliel, not inhaling quarry dust for most of his life. What had Saul done to earn such favor that had been kept from him?

He turned to face the Ark of Scrolls. His greatest desire lay behind the simple wooden doors. The opportunity had never been so close and yet so far away at the same moment.

When the room emptied of the rest of the teachers, Ethan moved toward him. "Be careful not to worship at the altar of scrolls."

Jude looked over his shoulder at the teacher.

"An important lesson all students of Torah must learn."

A scoff escaped Jude's mouth before he could stop it. There would be many lessons he wouldn't have the chance to learn.

Ethan stepped closer to the cabinet and patted the closed doors. "Contained within are the words given to us by Adonai. A precious resource we must guard and preserve. For we do not know if or when He will choose to speak again. It's been four hundred years since His last prophet."

"Adonai has said plenty that we are still trying to understand." Jude allowed his attention to return to the Ark. "And He has spoken again; in my brother. We just didn't know how to listen."

Ethan chuckled as he walked closer to Jude. "There is much potential in you."

Jude shook his head. A whole room full of teachers had extinguished that flame of hope in him.

Rabbi Ethan folded his hands behind his back and lifted his chin. "Follow me."

Jude's attention snapped to the man. "What did you say?"

"Follow me."

"But...but I thought you said you were not taking students."

"I cannot stand by and watch as a brilliant student remains unled."

Jude bounded up the bema and wrapped his arms around Ethan. "I will follow."

CHAPTER 3

With light steps, Jude raced back to the villa to share his good news with his siblings. The streets of Jerusalem were filled with people engaged in their everyday activities. The joy that flooded Jude's soul pressed him through the throng toward the priest's house in the Upper City he shared with his family and Jesus' followers.

He pushed open the heavy wooden door of Theodotos' villa and hurried to shut it behind him.

"Jude." The surprise was clear in Salome's voice. "How was the reading?"

The sting of embarrassment burned for a moment as Jude recalled the events of the morning, but the remembrance of his new status flamed his joy once more. "Sister," he crossed the mosaic tile of the entryway toward her, "I have great news."

She looked up at him with bright eyes.

Jude hesitated. His youngest sister's eyes were the same reflective hue of cinnamon as their oldest brother's. For a single moment, it was as if Jesus was looking out at him through Salome's eyes. He wondered if his brother would be proud of the path he'd chosen to take.

"Jude?"

"Forgive me," Jude shook his head. "I was just…"

The place between Salome's brows scrunched together.

Jude chuckled as he kissed the wrinkled spot on her forehead. "I have a Rabbi."

"Oh, Jude, that's wonderful." She clapped her hands. "Is it Rabbi Gamaliel?"

He pulled back, fighting the painful wound in his soul that the older teacher had left behind with his discouraging words. "Rabbi Ethan."

"I thought you said he wasn't taking students."

"He changed his mind."

Salome wavered for a moment. "Well, I'm sure you will be happy at his feet."

Jude kissed his youngest sister's forehead again. "I need to tell James." He moved toward the stairs.

"He's with Salvus." Salome pointed to the lower room. "I was on my way to fetch fresh water for him."

Jude adjusted his steps toward the room where the injured soldier was being kept. He entered to find James sitting next to the young man who was propped against the wall. A welcome sight from the previous days in which he'd been unable to sit up at all. The room was kept dim with a curtain over the small window. An oil lamp flickered near James, helping him to see to his caregiving tasks. The room smelled of sweat and musk. Signs the injured man still warred with his injury.

Jude moved to stand near them. "How are you feeling, Salvus?"

"Better." The soldier winced as he adjusted his wrapped leg. "But I fear how long I will be kept here."

Jude looked to James. "Has something happened?"

"Salvus was sharing his concern about returning to his unit." James indicated the man's wound with a tilt of his head. "He worries he will be punished for leaving."

"But he was injured." Jude dipped his head. "Surely they will be understanding."

"I'm certain they believe a disease has overtaken me by now." Salvus rubbed his thigh. "Some moments I wish the venom had done so."

Jude crouched down. "You can't mean that."

Salvus' face was damp with sweat. "I don't know what awaits me in Rome's grasp. At least the viper's kiss could have brought a final relief."

Jude settled into a seated position. "Is being a soldier such an awful fate that you'd rather taste death than return?"

"Depends. Mostly one's life is routine." Salvus winced again. "With the influx of soldiers into the city for the feast days, those of us who could afford to rent houses did so to make room at Fortress Antonia for those on temporary assignment. I was supposed to report back days ago." He massaged his thigh. "Don't know if the relocation was a blessing or a curse."

"You're alive," James offered.

"For how long is the question." Salvus laid his head against the stone wall. "I don't know what Longinus will do when he discovers me."

Salome entered with a bowl of freshly drawn water. She sat the vessel down next to the soldier and handed clean linens to James before leaving the room.

James dipped a cloth in the water and patted Salvus' forehead. "Your fever is breaking. Soon you will be well enough to report to your commander."

Salvus exhaled a ragged breath.

Jude rose to his feet. "We should let you get some rest."

After wiping away more sweat, James wrung out the cloth and laid it near the bowl. He stood and followed Jude out of the room.

When they walked a few paces away, Jude whispered, "Is he truly getting better?"

"Slowly." James nodded. "He simply needs more time to heal."

Jude glanced back at the open door. "Do you think removing the watch over him was wise?"

"I wanted to show him that we trust him."

"Do you?"

"I don't know." James turned to enter the courtyard. "Can we trust a Roman soldier?"

"Hiram didn't think so." Jude halted by the stone bench. "Have you heard from him?"

James shook his head. "Not since he stormed out of here the other day. Assia mentioned he had come to speak with me about something." He lowered himself to the bench as if a weight were pressing on him.

"Do you think Assia and Joseph have made it to Nazareth?"

"I'm sure they have by now."

Jude slid onto the bench next to his brother. "I can't believe we're missing our sister's wedding feast."

"I'm certain Hiskiel's family is attending to the details."

"That must be a load off your shoulders."

James folded his arms across his body. "One wheat head removed from a load is barely noticed by the ox."

Jude took in his older brother. The weight of responsibility was evident in his slumped shoulders and tired eyes. "There has been a lot placed on you recently, hasn't there?"

"There has." He hesitated. "But there are many to share the load."

Jude glanced around. "Where are the others?"

"Visiting." James relaxed his arms. "The women, too. Salome and I stayed behind to tend to Salvus. There are many in need here in Jerusalem. Some days I wonder if we are doing enough."

"There will always be those in need."

"Unfortunately." James let out a heavy sigh. "Perhaps I should visit Hiram at the market."

"I could accompany you if you'd like."

"I would appreciate the support." He rubbed the length of his face with his hand. "Oh, the reading. I nearly forgot. How did it go at the synagogue?"

Jude looked down at his sandals.

"That bad?"

"Not bad." Jude scratched at his beard. "Not great either. I did get a Rabbi; Ethan offered for me to follow him. But I believe I also confirmed in many elite minds today that I will never be respected among them."

"Don't be so hard on yourself." James placed a firm hand on Jude's shoulder. "Many of those same minds didn't respect Jesus and look how his following has grown."

"I'm not fond of taking a similar path if it leads to a Roman cross."

James hummed in agreement.

"I have a feeling I wouldn't be walking out of a tomb after three days as our brother did."

"Well," James slapped his leg, "when the others get back why don't you and I take a walk to the market and get some fresh air."

"I think that would be good for both of us." Jude rose. "I'm going to grab some food. I barely had the stomach to break my fast this morning."

James set his hands on the bench. "I think I'll sit

here a while and pray."

Making his way into the bustling kitchen, Jude found his mother stoking the fire. "Shalom, Ima."

"Jude." Her face brightened as she straightened. "How was the reading?"

Jude tried to keep his lips straight but one side slid up into a crooked grin. "Not as well as I would have liked but I was invited to sit at the feet of Ethan."

"Wonderful news. Here," she dipped a spoon into the pot over the fire and lifted it toward Jude, "try this and tell me what you think."

Jude opened his mouth as if he were a young child again receiving nourishment from his mother. The broth sent a welcomed warmth through him and awakened his taste. "It's good."

Mary smiled and returned her attention to her stew.

Wandering through the large kitchen, Jude picked at food in various stages of preparation.

Elissa sat on the ground grinding wheat kernels against a large stone.

"You should leave that task to Lydia," Jude teased his sister-in-law. "It's her favorite."

Lydia snapped a cloth in Jude's direction perfectly catching his arm.

"Ouch!"

"That's for making fun of me."

Jude rubbed his arm.

Elissa shook her head. "You had it coming, Jude. It's not kind to tease your sister."

With soft steps, he hovered over her work. "Well," he pulled her wrap from her head causing her long, dark hair to fall around her face, "I have enough sisters now to fill my days with jest." He dangled the material over her.

She snatched at the cloth nearly missing. "Jude."

He laughed as he waved the linen near her again.

"Give it back," Mary warned.

Jude shot an innocent glance at his mother. "Yes, Ima." He dropped the material into Elissa's open hand.

"Since you've so much free time," Mary crossed her arms, "why don't you go milk the goat."

"But Ima, I—"

Mary raised a strong brow at him.

"Yes, Ima." He lowered his shoulders and grabbed a vessel.

Lydia held the door open for him. "Say hello to Daniel for me."

Jude passed his smug sister on the way outside to where Theodotos kept his animals. His sister had taken pleasure in naming the collection with whom she spent her time. "At least my friends walk on two legs instead of four."

"Ugh!" Lydia swatted at him.

Jude chuckled all the way to his task.

CHAPTER 4

The late-day walk to the market did much to revive Jude's soul. He and James spoke of lighter topics as they made their way among the sellers sharing their wares.

When they reached Hiram's booth, Jude noticed a familiar form standing there. "What's Saul doing here?"

James bent around the crowd still moving between them and the tent. "Talia's brother Saul? Perhaps he is making a purchase."

Noticing the unfavorable scowl on Hiram's face and the man's large arms folded tightly against his chest allowed doubt to creep into Jude's mind. He pressed through the people. "Shalom, Hiram."

The tentmaker's attention snapped to him but he did not return the greeting.

Saul turned around to face Jude.

Jude noticed the same smirk on Saul's face that he carried from earlier that morning after the reading. The pang of embarrassment resurfaced in Jude.

Saul inclined his head. "Shalom to you both." With a grin still plastered on his face, he strode away into the market without another word.

"Are you well?" James asked Hiram.

"Yes." His gaze lingered on Saul's trail.

Jude stepped closer. "Do you know that man?"

"He's a fellow tentmaker," Hiram admitted through gritted teeth. "A serpent of a man if you ask me."

Jude perked up at the assessment. "Why do you say that?"

"He's always slithering around."

"What did he want?"

"Information."

"About?"

Hiram finally allowed his gaze to fall on Jude. "Way Followers."

Jude flinched. "What did you tell him?"

"Nothing." His stare lifted back to the crowd. "I didn't say anything to him."

Jude turned to James. "Why do you think he wanted information on Way Followers?"

"I know exactly why," Hiram interjected. "He's trying to get in good with the Sanhedrin. He thinks if he can bring them names, they will hasten his petition to be a Pharisee."

"He wants to be a Pharisee?"

Hiram nodded slowly. "He already has his teacher's recommendation and his father's status."

Jude tilted his head. "Then why is he vying for the

position?"

"His age." Hiram's arm muscles tightened. "The members of the Council think he's too young to be given an official seat. They want him to wait." He looked back at Jude. "Saul's not a patient man and desperate men are dangerous."

Jude felt acid rise in the back of his throat as the sickening glare of Saul's smug face hit his memory.

"He's also not married," James added. "I've heard the Pharisees are strict on that requirement as well."

"Usually," Hiram agreed. "Saul was betrothed before. His father was the one to break the agreement. Claimed the woman's family had been deceitful in their dealings. The accusation ruined them. They were forced to leave Jerusalem."

"Was it true?" Jude asked.

"Don't know." Hiram lifted a shoulder. "But there haven't been many other families lining up to give a daughter over to that viper. The other Pharisees have been very…_understanding_ on that point."

James cleared his throat. "We didn't come to speak about Saul. I'm here to see why you came to the villa the other day and why you haven't been back."

"Oh." Hiram dropped his arms to his sides. "It was nothing."

"Salome seemed to think it was important."

The large man's face flushed then shifted to red. "You still harboring that Roman dog?"

"The injured soldier is still in our care, yes."

"Then it doesn't matter what I had to say."

"Hiram, I've come to speak as a friend."

"No friend of mine would give aid to a Roman soldier. Especially one who tried to harm their own sister."

"He was mad with fever. Salome and Assia are both unharmed."

Jude's eyes traveled down the man's toned arm to the place a thin wrapping lay. Salvus had managed a slice into Hiram's flesh in his feverish fit though it seemed no permanent damage was done.

James closed the gap between them and lowered his voice, "'You shall love your neighbor as yourself.'"

Hiram's eyes closed into a tight line. "A good neighbor doesn't invade your home and kill the people you love."

Jude remembered the story Elissa had shared about Hiram's betrothed. She'd been abused and killed by a Roman soldier before their wedding feast. He couldn't imagine the depths of the man's pain. "Hiram?"

The tentmaker kept his eyes sealed.

"Hiram," Jude tried again. "I pray to Adonai that I never have to walk the path you've endured. But none of us can be considered a good neighbor. We denied our own brother." He motioned with his thumb between himself and James. "You've confessed to being a zealot. Would you have wanted Jesus to hold that charge against you?"

When Hiram opened his eyes, they glistened with unshed tears. "No."

"Then how can you hold Salvus' occupation against him?"

Hiram's jaw tightened.

"Besides, our brother didn't say to love only your good neighbors. Anyone can do that. He called us to love *all* of our neighbors. Even the not-so-good ones."

"What am I to do then?" Hiram flung his arms out. "Embrace that dog as a brother?"

Jude shot a pleading glance at James.

The older brother took the opening. "We don't expect you to do anything that Jesus wouldn't do for the man."

"He's not the soldier that killed your betrothed," Jude added.

Hiram's gaze dropped down to Jude.

Jude felt the icy look of disdain and realized he'd unintentionally struck a still-open wound.

"Away." Hiram brushed the air and turned his back to them. "Away."

Jude reached for him. "But—"

James set a hand on his brother's arm. "Let's give him some more time."

The two brothers left the market and headed back toward the villa.

"I didn't mean to say anything hurtful," Jude

started when the crowd thinned around them.

"I know." James kept his eyes on the street. "Hiram's wounds simply need more time to heal."

Jude recalled James' same assertion about Salvus' physical wound. He wasn't sure if time would be the cure for either man. He'd seen time harden instead of heal. He let the topic of Hiram drop in favor of another issue. "What about Saul?"

"What about him?"

Jude shrugged. "I mean what are we going to do about his search for Way Followers."

"Nothing."

"James," Jude stepped in front of his brother, "the man is seeking out those who followed Jesus. How much longer are you going to pretend he's not a threat to us?"

For several heartbeats, James simply stared at his brother. "I know very well Saul is a threat. So is Rome. And so is every other member of the council who doesn't agree with us." He let out a weighted breath. "But we can't hide away in fear or keep our brother's teachings to ourselves. Jesus spent three years of his life traveling and spreading the message of Adonai with as many people as he could." He put a brotherly hand on Jude's shoulder. "It's imperative that we continue that work. Even when there are those who would stand in our way."

Jude let his brother's words soak into his soul. "I

want to teach about our brother. Nothing would bring more joy to my life than to follow in Jesus' steps of sharing Adonai's message with the world." He shrugged off James' hand. "I simply don't want to dance in front of a viper's den while doing it."

James continued walking. "You're shaping into a fine student and I'm sure, with time, you'll be a great Rabbi."

Keeping up with his brother's steady pace, Jude considered James' encouragement. He couldn't remember a time before coming to Jerusalem this year that he'd heard James speak in favor of his dream. Many things had changed since they stepped foot in this city. His brother was a major one. "You think so?"

"I know so." James gave him a sideways glance before returning his attention to the path.

"With everything that happened to Jesus…" Jude hesitated to finish his thought.

"All the more reason for you to take up his mantle."

Jude pondered the idea. He remembered the prophet Elisha receiving the literal and symbolic mantle of his Rabbi, Elijah. The thought that Jesus left behind several of his disciples and followers with the command to spread the good news wrapped around him like an outer coat. Maybe James wouldn't make him go back to the quarry after all. If Jude continued to prove himself worthy, maybe, just maybe, he'd get to live out his dream in Jerusalem after all.

CHAPTER 5

A stream of sunlight poured in through the open door of Ethan's synagogue and made its way across the stone table in front of Jude. His back ached from being hunched over a scroll of Moses for most of the day.

His tired eyes burned as he re-read the section he'd been studying. *The Lord God took the man and put him in the garden of Eden to work it and keep it. And the Lord God commanded the man, saying, "You may surely eat of every tree of the garden, but of the tree of the knowledge of good and evil you shall not eat, for in the day when you eat of it you shall surely die.*

Ethan came to stand beside the table. "Starting at the beginning?"

Jude rubbed at his eyes. "I thought if there was one place Adonai spoke of His Anointed, surely I could find others. The beginning felt like a good place to start."

"And what have you found?"

With a light touch, Jude placed his finger on the word 'die.' He tapped the parchment. "Adonai told Adam not to eat of the tree of the knowledge of good and evil."

The teacher brushed his long, white beard with his

fingers. "But he did."

"He did, and it resulted in death." Jude studied the lines again. "Through a living tree, Adam brought forth death." His thoughts swirled. "Through a dead tree, Jesus brought forth life."

"Ahh." Ethan shook his finger in the air. "The wooden cross. You have been doing much meditation." He leaned over and pointed further on the scroll. "Have you made it here?"

Jude read aloud the words under his teacher's finger. "'I will put enmity between you and the woman, and between your seed and her seed; he shall bruise your head, and you shall bruise his heel.'" He looked up into Ethan's eyes. "Does that speak of Messiah as well?"

"Who else but Adonai's Anointed could crush the head of the serpent of lies and temptation?"

The smug face of Saul entered Jude's mind and transformed into a slithering serpent. He shook away the thought as his gaze washed over the words again. "'He shall bruise your head, and you shall bruise his heel.' A head wound would be fatal."

"So would a bite from a serpent. If left unattended," Ethan added.

Jude thought of Salvus' bite and what would have happened to him if his widowed neighbor had not found him and tended to his wound. He saw the words with fresh eyes. "Messiah had to die."

"'Shall I ransom them from the power of Sheol? Shall I redeem them from Death?'"

"'O Death, where are your plagues? O Sheol, where is your sting?'" Jude finished the line from the prophet Hosea. "Jesus had to die. But he took death with him."

"'He will swallow up death forever.'"

Jude tilted his head. The line sounded familiar but he couldn't recall the next.

"The prophet Isaiah. 'And the Lord God will wipe away tears from all faces, and the reproach of his people he will take away from all the earth, for the Lord has spoken.'"

"Adonai told us from the very beginning." Jude brushed his hands over the sacred words. "His plan all along for my brother."

"For all of us." Ethan stood straight. "'Your dead shall live; their bodies shall rise. You who dwell in the dust, awake, and sing for joy!'"

"Isaiah again?"

"Correct."

"Did he speak much of Messiah?"

"Oh," the old teacher chuckled, "a great many times."

Jude stretched his back. "I guess the prophet could have also been speaking of Hiram and the others who walked out of their tombs the same day Jesus did."

"Perhaps."

"You know, James and I visited Hiram yesterday."

"How is my friend?"

"I'm not sure." Jude shook his head. "He was ruffled."

His silver brow lifted. "Oh?"

"Saul was there." Jude waited for Ethan to react to the news. When the teacher remained impartial, he added, "Seeking Way Followers."

"I see."

Jude's attention dropped down to the scroll before him. "I wonder how many times Saul has been fortunate to drink from Adonai's words."

"He's been at Gamaliel's feet for years. I'm sure the two have studied many hours together."

"It doesn't seem fair." Jude caressed the marks on the parchment. "My whole life all I've wanted is to sit in a place like this unrolling scroll after scroll. Instead, I've choked on limestone dust and labored for my family to barely keep food in their stomachs. While I've been repeatedly denied, Saul has a seat among the Pharisees waiting for him as soon as he's old enough...and married."

"Well, that will not hold him back much longer."

Jude's forehead scrunched. "Why do you say that?"

"I've heard his father has signed a betrothal agreement for him."

Jude couldn't believe his hearing. After what Hiram had told him of the family who had been victim to their previous accusations, he wondered if Saul would ever have his own wedding feast. "Truly?"

Ethan's head bobbed. "A woman from a very wealthy family as I hear it. I believe the match will do much to promote his status."

He agreed with a groan. Uniting with a wealthy family would only add pull with the Council on Saul's behalf. He would gain the esteemed seat among the Pharisees soon. The idea made Jude sick to his stomach.

"The day is fading." Ethan moved to roll up the scroll. "Get some rest."

Jude's eyes burned once more reminding him of the long hours he'd been studying. Rest sounded good.

That night held Jude in a tight grip. He tossed upon his sleeping mat as darkness haunted him. A figure came forth from the dim. As the form sharpened, he realized it was Arava. She stood looking up.

Jude tried to call for her but his lips were sealed like a tomb.

A flash exploded above her revealing a blazing, orange tongue. He'd seen the same appear above the heads of his brother's followers only days ago. This one moved closer to Arava and lapped at her head. The flame grew so bright, Jude was forced to shield his eyes.

The light engulfed her as she opened her mouth. "My lips will pour forth praise, for You teach me Your statutes."

Jude recognized the familiar psalm. Arava was singing a song of their people.

"My tongue will sing of Your word, for all Your commandments are right."

Her voice was as beautiful as any Jude had ever heard.

"My lips will pour forth praise," Arava continued singing. "My tongue will sing of Your word."

When Jude attempted to reach out for her, the light shattered into darkness.

He sat straight up in the upper room of the villa with sweat dripping from his hair.

Arava. Her name danced in his thoughts. *Adonai, how can the deaf and mute sing?*

You who dwell in the dust, awake, and sing for joy! The words of Isaiah and his Rabbi came echoing back to him.

Jude wiped at his face and studied the forms around him.

His family lay peacefully sleeping. Their varied breathing formed a musical rhythm.

Quietly, he adjusted himself upon his mat and bowed his head. *Show me how to sing of Your word. Teach me to sing for joy. I don't know your path for Arava but show me how to be a good neighbor to her family. Even though my thoughts have not been kind toward her brother, Saul, show me Your ways. Keep me humble and ever a student of Your word. Thank you for Ethan and Your scrolls. Provide me the courage to speak and opportunities to do so.*

With peace refreshing his anxious heart, Jude laid down on his mat and closed his eyes. Arava's song of praise lulled him back to sleep.

CHAPTER 6

Jude shadowed James toward the Temple the following morning. He couldn't shake the dream of Arava but had no desire to share the vision with his siblings.

Peter and James had divided the followers into groups of two that morning. Their task was to make as many visits around the city as they could before the ninth hour. Then, they would meet in the Temple for prayer and teaching.

Much to Jude's dismay, James had insisted he pair with him this day. Jude wanted to spend another day pouring over scrolls, but James had other plans for him.

The two had made three visits ensuring widows had meals, injured men had extra hands to give them aid, and new followers knew where to meet for prayer and to hear from the disciples.

As Jude and James approached the Beautiful Gate, Jude asked, "Do you see the others?"

"I think that's Peter and John there." James motioned with his chin toward the gate. "I'm sure the others will be along shortly."

As they neared, Jude heard a man who lay at the

gate cry out, "Coins." He hesitated behind his brother.

The older man's legs were twisted like gnarled tree limbs. His arms stretched out ready to receive any charity the people would sacrifice but his head hung low. He kept his gaze away from those who passed him multiple times a day.

Peter stopped in front of the man.

"Coins," he called again, his voice as knotted as his legs. "Spare a coin."

"Look at us."

Jude recognized Peter's commanding voice. The same tone he used when he addressed a crowd.

The lame man's eyes came up with hesitation.

"I have no silver or gold," Peter's gaze was fixed on the man's face, "but what I do have I give to you. In the name of Jesus of Nazareth, rise and walk!" He reached out his right hand to the man.

As the man's legs came up under him, they became straight.

Jude couldn't believe his eyes. He rubbed his vision clear but when he looked again, the gnarled legs were as straight and strong as Lebanon cedars.

The man looked down at his legs and then back at Peter. "Praise Adonai!" He leapt around Peter and John. "Praise the God of Israel."

John stepped through the Beautiful Gate as Peter and James followed.

Jude hurried after them.

The man trailed, continuing to shout, "Praise Adonai!" He clung to Peter's outercoat. "Praise the God of Israel!"

The Temple crowd took notice of the commotion and gathered to discover the source.

One man stopped beside them. "Isn't that the beggar who asks for coins outside the gate?"

"Can't be," the woman next to him answered. "The beggar's legs are twisted. This man leaps on healthy legs."

"I'm certain that's him."

"How can that be?"

"Praise the God of Israel." The former lame man twirled around them.

Peter and John moved toward Solomon's portico where the group had agreed to gather for the hour of prayer.

Curious people followed them as they moved.

Jude struggled to keep up with James as the crowd pressed in around them.

"Did the men from Galilee heal him?" someone shouted.

"How can they heal anyone?" another man answered.

Peter turned toward the crowd. "Men of Israel, why do you wonder at this? Why do you stare at us?"

Jude glanced around as the crowd calmed to listen.

"Do you believe we have done this by our own

power or virtue?" Peter paused as he searched the gathering. "The God of Abraham, the God of Isaac, and the God of Jacob, the God of our fathers, glorified his servant Jesus, whom you delivered over and denied in the presence of Pilate, when he had decided to release him. But you denied the Holy and Righteous One, and asked for a murderer to be granted to you instead."

Jude felt the burn of anger in his chest. Recalling the freedom of Barabbas who still hunted in the city made his stomach turn. If the rumors were true, if Simon stalked beside him, he wondered how long it would be before Simon carried the same title of murderer.

"You killed the Author of life," Peter's voice rang out in the open porch, "whom Adonai raised from the dead. To this we are witnesses. And His name, by faith in His name, has made this man strong." He waved to the beggar who had been healed. "Faith in Jesus has given this man perfect health in the presence of you all." He moved his hand toward the people. "Brothers, I know that you acted in ignorance, as did also your rulers. What Adonai foretold by the mouth of all the prophets, that his Christ would suffer, Jesus has fulfilled."

"What should we do?" a man cried out.

"Repent!" Peter demanded. "Turn back, that your sins may be blotted out, that times of refreshing may come from the presence of the Lord, and that he may send the Christ appointed for you, Jesus, whom heaven must receive until the time for restoring all things about which Adonai spoke by the mouth of His holy prophets long ago."

Jude considered the piles of scrolls locked away in the cabinet in Ethan's synagogue. He hungered to study the words of the prophets. They spoke of Messiah, and Jude had not seen Him revealed in his own brother.

He wondered at how a lowly fisherman was able to speak about such findings with only a few years of lessons as a boy and a few more with his brother. Had Jesus shared about the prophets with his followers before he died? Why had he not shared as much with his own brother knowing the depth of his heart?

Peter met Jude's gaze as if reading his thoughts. "Moses said, 'The Lord God will raise up for you a prophet like me from your brothers. You shall listen to him in whatever he tells you. And it shall be that every soul who does not listen to that prophet shall be destroyed from the people.' And all the prophets who have spoken, from Samuel and those who came after him, also proclaimed these days."

As people gathered closer to Peter, Jude noticed a group of men rushing toward them. He reached over and put a hand on James' shoulder.

James turned toward him.

Jude pointed to the group heading their way.

"They don't look happy."

"No, they don't." Jude watched a collection of priests, Sadducees, and even the captain of the Temple guard move in their direction.

One of the priests led the way and stopped short in front of Peter. "What is the meaning of your words?"

"We speak of Jesus," Peter answered.

"You speak lies," a Sadducee called over him. "Adonai does not raise men from the dead."

People murmured around them.

Peter looked at the crowd. "You are the sons of the prophets and of the covenant that Adonai made with your fathers, saying to Abraham, 'And in your offspring shall all the families of the earth be blessed.' Adonai, having raised up His servant, sent Jesus to you first, to bless you by turning every one of you from your wickedness."

"Lies!" The Sadducee moved toward Peter. "Arrest this false prophet."

The Temple captain pushed through the crowd.

"Repent!" Peter cried out. "Repent!"

John stepped to his side.

James turned away and shoved Jude. "We need to leave, now!"

Jude stumbled over his sandals as the people scattered in all directions. He kept his eyes over his shoulder as he watched the guard bind Peter and John.

"Move!" James demanded.

With hesitation, Jude faced forward and ran in the direction of the villa.

CHAPTER 7

Jude didn't slow down until he made it to Theodotos' villa. When he and James were safely inside, they secured the door.

Salome came into the entryway at the sound of their entrance. "What happened?" She examined her brothers. "You're covered in sweat."

Jude leaned his back against the door attempting to catch his breath. "Better than chains."

"Chains?" Salome shrieked.

James moved toward her. "Peter and John have been arrested.

"On what charges?"

"They were teaching about Jesus in the Temple."

She looked between him and Jude. "Go upstairs. I'll fetch you some water and something to eat."

James stopped her. "Tell the servants not to open this door for anyone but followers we already know."

Salome nodded slowly and rushed toward the kitchen.

Andrew arrived in the entryway. "James, is that you?"

James nodded. "Jude and I are here. Where are the

others?"

"Nathanael and I were the first ones back. What became of my brother?"

"Peter and John were both arrested."

Andrew pushed past them.

James grabbed ahold of his tunic. "Picking a fight with the Council isn't going to result in anything but you sharing a cell with your brother."

"I'd gladly be found there if it were my fate."

The door rattled behind Jude.

Jude pushed off it as James stepped closer. "Reveal yourself."

"It is I, Philip."

James lifted the beam and opened the door.

Several men piled into the entrance.

Thomas was the last one in. "Secure the door."

Jude helped James reposition the heavy beam into place. "Did everyone make it back?"

Thomas turned to Andrew. "Philip and I arrived at Solomon's portico just as Peter and John were being arrested."

James looked around the group. "Where's Matthias?"

"Peter assigned him watch over Salvus," Andrew answered.

"Jude and I will inform him of what happened." James moved toward the lower rooms. "The servants have been instructed not to answer the door for anyone we don't know. As for the rest of you, everyone is to remain inside. Go upstairs and pray. My brother and I will join you soon."

Jude followed James toward the room of their unintended guest.

Matthias was in the process of changing the soldier's bandage.

Jude took in the man. Color had returned to his face, and he seemed to have final victory over the fever. Even the old wrappings sitting near Matthias contained far less infection than in previous days.

James knelt beside him. "How are you, Salvus?"

"One day deeper in debt with Rome."

"Salvus," James' voice shook. "I need to ask you a question."

The man stared up at him, his brows knitting together.

"Two of our friends were arrested today."

Matthias stilled his hands. "Who?"

"Peter and John," James answered him reluctantly before he turned back to Salvus. "Do you know what will happen to them?"

Salvus looked to Matthias, then to Jude before returning his attention to James. "If you think I can help them escape—"

"No." James put up a hand. "Nothing like that. I simply want to know what is happening to them."

"It all depends on who arrested them."

James looked up at Jude.

"A captain of the Temple guard." By his dress and decoration, Jude was sure of the man's position.

"Uzzi."

Jude knelt. "You know him?"

"Not personally." Salvus flinched as Matthias secured the wrap on his leg. "But I've dealt with the Temple guard many times before."

James tried his question again. "What do they do to their prisoners?"

"They'd be counted fortunate it wasn't a Roman who bound them. They would have found no favor as a prisoner of Rome." The soldier rubbed his thigh. "If the Temple guard took them, they'd be kept under the Temple in the common prison until they could be taken before Caiaphas."

"When?"

"Tomorrow." Salvus leaned back against the wall. "The day is far too gone to call a gathering."

"You're sure."

"Positive." He let out a heavy breath. "One thing you Jews are good at is keeping your traditions."

Jude rose to his feet along with James. "They didn't keep those traditions with Jesus. They had no problem calling an unofficial trial in the middle of the night to try to sway the procedures."

James pulled at his beard. "Let's hope Peter and John are far less prized fish hanging at the end of their lines."

"James," Andrew called from the doorway, "come quickly."

James shared a disheartening glance with Jude before leaving the room.

"Rest, Salvus," Jude encouraged. "Thank you for your help." He hurried to follow his brother.

James stood with Andrew in the open area leading to the entryway. "Say that again."

"People." Andrew pointed to the door. "Ria says there is a crowd outside demanding to see us."

"Guards?"

Andrew shook his head. "She said they were just ordinary people but a whole group of them."

Jude came up next to his brother. "What do you think they want?"

"I don't know if it's safe to find out." James rubbed at his temple.

"The servant said the people were persistent," Andrew added. "She tried to send them away but they are still out there in the street."

"Gather the others," James ordered. "Jude and I will discover their intentions." He moved toward the door.

Jude followed with his heart beating wildly in his chest. He didn't have any skills to combat a crowd. What help could he offer his brother?

James removed the beam from the door and

stepped outside.

Jude trailed him and pulled the door closed behind them.

A multitude of people stood waiting for them just as Ria had claimed.

James addressed them, "Whom do you seek?"

"The men of Galilee," someone deep in the crowd shouted.

"Why?" James asked.

"We heard the one called Peter speak at the Temple."

"We have questions."

"Is it true he was arrested?"

"How can we have our sins blotted out?"

The questions came quickly at the two brothers.

James held up his hands. "Peace."

Jude looked at the growing group. He couldn't count the number. They all looked frightened and lost like sheep without a shepherd.

James lowered his arms. "It is true that both Peter and John have been arrested by the Temple Guard for speaking of Jesus."

"Is it true that Jesus of Nazareth's name can be used to heal?" a voice cried out.

James looked at Jude. "Open the door."

"But James, there are so many and we have Salvus inside. What if they discover him?"

"Open the door."

Jude turned around and pushed on the large wooden door. The hinges groaned in protest.

"Come inside and have your questions answered." James led the way into the villa.

Jude held the door open.

The crowd poured in behind them as the disciples were descending the stairs.

Jude caught eyes with Andrew as the open area flooded with people.

James moved toward the men. "These people have questions about what Peter was teaching today. We need to share with them about Jesus."

"Of course."

The men filtered through the crowd answering one question after another. People sat in small groups all around the villa as the large gathering came and went for hours. Those unable to fit inside the enclosed space of the villa patiently waited their turn in the streets. The constant flow of people in an out of the structure reminded Jude of a port city. He wondered when if the number would ever diminish.

Jude moved from group to group answering questions as best he could and taught of all that Jesus had done and spoken.

By the time the last person left the villa, the evening had grown late and the men had grown tired.

When the door was secure for the night, James turned to Matthew. "Well, friend, how many?"

The former tax collector raised a curious brow at him.

"I know you kept count."

"Five thousand."

Jude felt his knees tremble. "Did you say five thousand?"

"I made my count twice." He showed the marks on his scroll as evidence. "And that was just the men."

Jude turned toward his brother. "Five thousand men."

"Praise Adonai."

"Praise indeed," Jude answered. "But we've barely been able to see to the needs of those in our care already. How are we going to help another five thousand families?"

"That's not our problem to solve." James staggered away on tired legs toward the upper room.

Jude watched his brother and the other men head to their waiting sleeping mats. *How Adonai? Jesus could multiply fish and bread. We can barely answer all of their questions. How are we to supply for so great a need?*

CHAPTER 8

"Jude."

Jude opened his eyes to see James above him. He blinked in the darkness. "What is it?"

"Come on."

He sat up. "Where are we going?"

"The Temple." James threw a clean tunic at him. "We need to see what will become of Peter and John."

"It's barely daybreak."

"I don't want to miss the gathering of the council." James adjusted a clean tunic over his head. "Wash your face too."

"Are you going to allow me to break my fast?"

"On the way." He headed for the door. "Get ready, and I'll meet you downstairs."

Jude pulled off the tunic he'd spent the last few days in, cleaned himself the best he could, and slipped into the fresh garment.

He hurried through his morning recitations as he prepared. *I give thanks unto You, Adonai, that, in mercy, You have restored my soul within me. Endless is Your compassion; great is Your faithfulness. I thank You, Adonai, for the rest You have given me through the night and for the breath that renews my body and spirit. May I renew my soul with faith in You, source of all healing. Blessed are You, Adonai our God, Ruler of the Universe, Who renews daily the work of creation.*

He tied on his sandals and found James waiting for him by the front door.

James tossed him a folded cloth.

Jude opened it to find some dried fruit. He ate it as they made their way across Jerusalem to the Temple.

Devoted men were already gathering for the day while merchants set up to trade.

"Hurry," James urged as he headed toward the Chamber of Hewn Stone. "The Council will be gathering soon."

Jude followed his brother into the semi-circle room and waited toward the back. He watched as the seats at the front filled with scribes, elders, and members of the Great Sanhedrin. Then the man who Peter had healed was brought forward and set to the side.

The seat in the center remained empty until a group of men entered. Annas led his son-in-law, Caiaphas, and his two sons, Johnathan and Alexander, into the meeting and took the center chair.

Jude leaned over to James. "Why is Annas in the Nasi seat?"

"I don't know," James answered.

"Looks like most of the high priestly family is present." Jude motioned to the men behind the former High Priest with his chin.

"No doubt they are in training on how to properly conduct trials," James mused.

"But Caiaphas has been High Priest for years. He was appointed by Valerius Gratus."

"And his father-in-law has sat many times in the judgment seat anyway."

Annas motioned to the guard.

A door on the side opened. Peter and John were led in, still bound, and were positioned to stand before Annas.

"By what power or by what name did you do this?" Annas' voice boomed around the room.

Peter spoke first, "Rulers of the people and elders."

Jude recognized his tone immediately. It was the same bold and powerful one he often used when he wanted his voice heard by a crowd.

"If we are being examined today concerning a good deed done to a crippled man, by what means this man has been healed, let it be known to all of you and to all the people of Israel that by the name of Jesus of Nazareth, whom you crucified, whom Adonai raised from the dead—by Him this man is standing before you well." Peter waved with his bound hands to the man standing off to the side.

The gathering's attention turned momentarily

toward the formerly lame man.

He stood as still as a Roman statue gazing upward.

Peter continued, "This Jesus is the stone that was rejected by you, the builders," his chains rattled as he moved his hands toward Annas and the others, "which has become the cornerstone. And there is salvation in no one else, for there is no other name under heaven given among men by which we must be saved."

Jude watched Caiaphas lean forward to whisper in Annas' ear.

The rest of the Council also murmured among themselves.

Annas flicked his fingers toward Peter and John.

The guards pushed the two men back through the side door.

Johnathan leaned forward toward his father. "What shall we do with these men?"

"A notable sign has been performed through them and is evident to all the inhabitants of Jerusalem," Alexander added. "We cannot deny it."

Caiaphas nodded.

Annas straightened in his seat. "In order that this may spread no further among the people, let us warn them to speak no more to anyone in this name."

The three men behind him nodded in approval.

With a wave of his hand, Annas recalled Peter and John.

When the fishermen stood before them again,

Annas commanded, "You are not to speak or teach at all in the name of Jesus."

John stepped forward. "Whether it is right in the sight of Adonai to listen to you rather than to Him, you must judge, for we cannot help but speak of what we have seen and heard."

"You must hold your tongue," Annas charged him. "Do not teach about the raising of the dead and do not speak of Jesus anymore."

The former lame man moved closer. "Adonai has done great works through these men and their Rabbi. More need to hear of what has been done."

Annas glanced around the room as the Council spoke in hushed tones behind up held hands with one another. He flicked a cautious gaze at the three men behind him before returning his attention to Peter and John. "On account of this man's testimony, and finding no wrong doing, I release you."

Peter and John shared a grateful look among themselves.

"But," Annas added, "be warned. Do not speak or teach of this Jesus of Nazareth again." He waved them away.

The guards unbound their hands and allowed them to leave.

As they made their way to the back of the room, James came up beside them. "Thank Adonai you've been freed."

"Did you see the look on Annas' face when that beggar stepped forward?" John asked.

"He couldn't deny the testimony," Jude explained. "The man is of sufficient age to testify before the council."

"Come," James motioned to them, "let's get out of here before they change their minds.

Jude looked back to see the four men staring at them. A shiver ran up his spine at their warning glare.

When they made it back to the villa, Peter gathered the others together and shared about what had happened to them.

"And they just let you go?" Andrew asked after listening to the tale.

"There was nothing more they could do," John answered.

Peter gazed upward. "Sovereign Lord, who made the heaven and the earth and the sea and everything in them, who through the mouth of our father David, your servant, said by the Holy Spirit, 'Why did the Gentiles rage, and the people plot in vain? The kings of the earth set themselves, and the rulers were gathered together, against the Lord and against his Anointed'— for truly in this city there were gathered together against your holy servant Jesus, whom you anointed, both Herod and Pontius Pilate, along with the Gentiles and the peoples of Israel, to do whatever Your hand and Your plan had predestined to take place."

Jude marveled at the fisherman. The uneducated, common man spoke as if he'd spent every day of his life at the feet of Adonai's Anointed. Jude chuckled to himself. He knew the men had spent three years with Jesus but didn't know how much they had learned from his brother. Peter simply opened his mouth and out tumbled grand words worthy of any Rabbi's tongue. He wondered if such a gift would be granted to him one day as well.

"And now, Lord," Peter continued his prayer, "look upon their threats and grant to Your servants to continue to speak Your word with all boldness, while You stretch out Your hand to heal, and signs and wonders are performed through the name of Your holy servant Jesus."

At the name of his brother, Jude felt the ground under them shake. It was as familiar as the day the tongues appeared. He glanced up hoping to see them once again. But the air above them remained still.

When the shaking ceased, a warm sense of peace and power filled him. He knew it was Adonai's Spirit. It was the same as when the tongue had rested upon him but this time no flaming sign from the heavens was needed. His body tingled at the surge. Something more was coming; he could feel it. He prayed he would be ready for what was next.

CHAPTER 9

The following morning started with a knock on the door which continued relentlessly.

Jude came downstairs to people in the villa speaking with James and the disciples.

"Who are all these people?" Jude questioned his brother.

"Men from all over." James motioned with his head toward the growing crowd. "Some from last night have come back."

"With more questions?" Jude's teacher's heart bloomed with hope.

"Some. But most have come with funds." James held up a money pouch and shook it.

Jude heard the distinct rattle of silver and tilted his head. "Funds?"

"It seems Adonai's Spirit was busy last night pressing these people to sell houses and land and to bring us the proceeds. We have much more resources now to distribute to those in need."

Jude glanced around to see money pouches being freely handed over. He'd never seen so many coins be exchanged outside of the Temple or the market. The incredible act brought his brother to his mind. "Do you think Joseph was successful in selling our house and land in Nazareth?"

James took a moment to consider the question. "I'm sure Adonai has given him wisdom."

"I hope he returns soon."

James looked around the open area at the large crowd. "So do I. We could use the extra hands."

"How can I help?"

"Why don't you check on Salvus? I don't think anyone has tended him yet."

Jude nodded. He moved carefully through the group to the lower-level room they used to care for the injured soldier.

As Jude pushed the door open, he saw Salvus upright for the first time since they carried him into the villa. "Feeling better this morning?"

"Well enough." Salvus slapped his wrapped thigh. "I must be returning." He took a step but stumbled forward.

Jude reached out to steady him. "You can barely walk. Are you sure you wouldn't rather rest for another day or so until you are more fully recovered?"

"I can't afford any more hospitality." He stabilized himself. "I must face what lies ahead."

"You don't even know what waits for you."

"No soldier does," he admitted. "That doesn't stop us."

"At least allow us to fashion you a staff." He pointed toward the mat. "My brothers and I are skilled craftsmen. We could carve you one in no time."

"I'm indebted enough already to my hosts."

Jude hesitated. "You owe us no debt."

Salvus looked him up and down. "Of course I do. You've provided shelter, food, and medical treatment for days. As soon as I return to my position and am able to earn a wage again, I will be sure to—"

"You don't owe us anything," Jude repeated with more force.

The Roman stood still for several heartbeats. "I don't understand."

"What we did for you," Jude explained, "we did because we believe in caring for those in need." He moved toward the door and pointed. "Right now, dozens of men stand in this villa with money pouches full of coins from the sale of their homes and lands. Funds that will be used to help people in need just like you."

Salvus' attention drifted toward the open doorway. "Why?"

"Because Adonai told them to."

"Who's Adonai?"

"Adonai is the one, true God. He is the One we worship and the One who sent Messiah, my brother, to save us."

One of Salvus' eyebrows came up. "Your brother is

a god?"

"No, well yes, well..." Jude rubbed his forehead with the thick part of his palm. "I'm sorry. I'm not very good at this."

Salvus waited for him to continue.

"Why don't you sit for a moment, and I will explain everything." He waved again toward the sleeping mat.

"I really need to report back to the Fortress."

"Please." Jude motioned again. "I will be as brief as possible."

Salvus sighed as he eased slowly to the ground.

Jude knelt beside him as he had done several times over the past few days. He took a steadying breath and lifted a quick prayer for Adonai's Spirit to help his words flow with clarity and power. "I know you Romans believe in many gods. We Hebrews believe in one." He lifted a single finger for emphasis. "One God who created the heavens and the earth. One God who poured Himself into human flesh."

"How could he still be a god if he became a man?"

Jude had wrestled with the same thing himself as he studied about Messiah. It was a complex idea that had been beyond his reach. He decided to share his best attempt at an explanation, "If you take a vessel to the sea and fill it up, have you emptied the sea?"

Salvus thought for a moment. "Well, no."

"But if you taste the water from that vessel, you'd know from where it had been gathered, right?"

"I suppose."

"I believe it was the same with Adonai when He sent Messiah. He poured some of Himself into flesh. Not completely emptying Himself but providing enough to reveal who He was." Jude shook his head. "I didn't believe my brother was Messiah either...at first. I lived with him all my life and didn't realize it." He ran his fingers in the dust on the floor. "I should have. He fulfilled all the prophecies concerning the Anointed One."

"Even if your brother was sent by a god, what does that have to do with the people out there," he flicked his chin toward the door, "or me?"

Jude's head rose slowly. "Everything." He settled into a seated position. "Salvus, it has everything to do with you. My brother came for people like you."

"Romans?" He sneered.

"Romans, Hebrews, Gentiles...everyone. He died to blot out our sins. He rose from the dead to save us. His blood was shed as payment for our sins."

"And what if we don't need saving?"

Jude's gaze traveled to the soldier's hand. It was shaking. "We all need a Savior. Some of us just don't know it yet." He lifted his eyes to Salvus' face. "I didn't know I needed one either. But I did, and so do you."

"Well," he groaned as he stood with much difficulty, "I must be returning to the Fortress."

"Stay." Jude jumped to his feet. "Stay here where

we can protect you."

Salvus leaned on his good leg. "No one can be protected from Rome. When that wolf wants you, she'll find you." He limped toward the door. "It's best not to run when she's on the hunt."

Jude easily kept up with him. "Adonai can protect you."

Salvus hesitated at the doorway. "Gods only protect their own." He stepped out into the open area. "No Hebrew god would care enough to protect a Roman soldier."

Jude watched him head toward the main door. His wrapped leg almost dragged along behind him. The soldier kept his back straight and his head up all the way through the door and out into the streets of Jerusalem.

With a sigh of defeat, Jude leaned against the stone wall. His words had failed another person. His heart felt like a boulder in his chest. The warmth of Adonai's Spirit withdrew in him like rain clouds in a drought. *Draw Salvus to Yourself, Adonai, as only You can. I know I still have much to learn. Help me teach about Your Anointed.*

As Jude kept his gaze on the open door, his hopes of adding Salvus to the mounting number of Way Followers was carried away with the wind. He wondered if his path would ever cross with the warrior again. A shudder went through him at the thought of being held in his charge as a prisoner of Rome as Jesus had endured only months earlier. With every breath in his lungs, he wanted another chance to speak with him but hoped it wouldn't be with his hands bound.

CHAPTER 10

James came over and put a hand on Jude's shoulder. "Brother?"

Jude opened his eyes to see the concern on his face.

"Was that Salvus who left?"

Jude nodded.

"Are you well?"

He lifted a shoulder but held his tongue.

"Why don't you come help the others."

Jude glanced at the front door and then turned to his brother and nodded. He pushed off the wall and followed him to where a few men remained.

Peter stood with Andrew. The two were speaking with a man that Jude recognized from the previous night.

He held out a money pouch toward Peter. "This is the full profit from the sale of my land."

The fisherman accepted the bag and handed it to Andrew without looking inside.

Jude saw something wash over Peter's face, a darkness. Something troubled him.

The man turned to leave.

"Ananias," Peter called.

Jude recognized the shift in Peter's voice. The tone meant he was getting ready to say something of great importance.

"Why has the Adversary filled your heart to lie to the Holy Spirit and to keep back for yourself part of the proceeds of the land?"

Jude's attention shifted to the man.

Ananias opened his mouth to speak, but no words came forward.

"While the land remained unsold, did it not remain your own?" Peter asked. "And after it was sold, was it not at your disposal?"

Ananias' bottom jaw shook but no words made their way forward.

"Why is it that you have contrived this deed in your heart?" Peter shook his head. "You have not lied to man, but to God."

Ananias fell to the ground.

The men next to Jude stood frozen. Jude's own feet felt adhered to his spot as he stared at the motionless body on the ground. Jude kept an eye on Ananias as he slowly made his way toward him. He knelt and placed his palm over Ananias' mouth. No air moved in or out. His fingers trembled at the realization. "He's dead."

"Dead?" Andrew turned to Peter.

Peter hung his head. "Take him outside the city and bury him."

Andrew moved to stand in front of his brother.

"Peter, what are you saying?"

"Adonai has judged. Take him out and bury him." He turned toward the stairs and ascended them with cautious steps.

Dead. The single word rang through Jude's mind. One moment alive, the next dead. He remembered those of their ancestors who had touched the Ark of Covenant and been struck dead where they stood. This man had lied. Adonai had judged. Jude's skin pricked all over.

James knelt beside Jude. "Get a blanket."

Jude rose on weak legs and rushed to where the women kept the clean linens. He snatched a blanket from the pile and returned to the group.

Working together, James, Andrew, and Jude wrapped the body tight. They lifted Ananias onto their shoulders and made their way out of the villa and headed south. With purposeful steps, they passed through the Dung Gate out of the city toward the Hinnom Valley.

Jude shivered against the heat of the day and the sand that scratched his skin with the winds. His gaze brushed the west. In the distance, he knew there stood a hill upon which his brother had died. The valley ahead of them was a common place to dispose of bodies and refuse alike. The never-ending flames licked at the air releasing their warmth toward them.

Andrew halted. "Here."

"Here?" Jude asked. "Why not put him in the flames?"

"Peter said to bury him."

The three lowered the body to the ground.

Andrew picked a spot and started pushing the sand to one side.

James knelt to do the same.

Jude fell to his knees as the sand gave way under him. He pushed the warm earth aside, carving out the final resting place of Ananias. His thoughts drifted to the stone tomb of Joseph of Arimathea that stood in a garden on the west side of the city. The large cave that had held his brother for only three days was now empty again. The rich could afford such luxuries. The poor were mostly forced to choose the ground or the flames.

As the sun crawled above them, they worked to create a deep enough hole. They slid Ananias' body into the opening and pushed the loose sand over him. When they had sufficiently completed their task, they made their way back to the villa.

Jude entered to find the open area emptied of the men from earlier. He couldn't blame them. He'd have left too if he saw someone drop dead after handing over a money pouch. What must they have thought? He still wrestled with the terrifying event and what it meant.

With hunger clawing his midsection, he went to the kitchen to find something to eat.

The large room clamored as it did most of the time.

His mother and sisters, along with the house servants, fluttered around the room as if locked in a daily dance. Food was in a constant state of preparation, and there were always some household tasks that needed doing.

"Jude," Mary greeted him warmly with a smile and a pat on the cheek.

"Ima." He kissed her cheek and moved toward his sister.

Salome was cutting a large cucumber.

Jude pointed toward the fire and, when she turned away, he snatched a slice and put it in his mouth.

She turned back to him and realized his mouth was full. Looking down at her work, she discovered the missing piece. "Jude." She playfully smacked his arm. "If you are hungry, all you had to do was ask."

He rubbed his arm. "Sister, I seek sustenance," he teased as he held out his hand.

She glanced down. "After you wash. Your hands are filthy."

Jude looked at his rough hands. They were still covered with sand.

"What have you been doing?"

He kept his gaze on his hands. He didn't want to answer her question. The truth would be hard to explain. Something he didn't even understand.

Without addressing her concern, he moved toward the washing vessel and dipped his hands in. He poured water up his arms and scrubbed the sand away. He lifted his hands and shook off the dripping water. Reaching for a rag, he dried his hands and went back to Salome.

She paused her chopping.

Jude lifted his hands for her inspection.

"Better." She gave him a bowl of sliced cucumbers and dried figs.

He gratefully accepted the vessel and went back into the open area.

A knock came at the door before he reached the bottom of the bowl. He answered the knocking to discover a woman standing there. "May I help you?"

"I'm searching for my husband." She twisted her fingers. "He came here a few hours ago seeking Peter."

"What's his name?"

"Ananias."

Jude's stomach dropped. "Come in." He moved so she could enter. "I'll take you to Peter." He escorted her to the room where Peter, James, and Andrew were praying. "Peter?"

Peter looked up at him.

"This is Ananias' wife..." Jude turned to her. "I'm sorry, I didn't get your name."

"Sapphira." She attempted a slight smile.

Peter's gaze moved from her to his brother and then on to James.

The two men moved toward the door to give her an audience with Peter.

Jude stayed back by the door with the others.

"Tell me, Sapphira," Peter paced, "did your husband sell a piece of land for fifteen pieces of silver?"

"Yes," her voice held a slight tremor. "Fifteen pieces."

Peter stopped and turned to face her. "How is it that you and your husband have agreed together to test the Spirit of the Lord? Behold, the feet of those who have buried your husband are at the door, and they will carry you out."

Jude watched Sapphira fall to the ground in the place her husband had only hours before.

Peter held his head. "Bury her beside her husband."

Jude looked at James.

James quietly shook his head.

"I'll get a blanket."

CHAPTER 11

A little over a week after Salvus' departure, Jude found himself thinking of the soldier. His thoughts drifted to the monstrous Fortress of Antonia to the north that housed his former houseguest. They had received no word from him since his sudden choice to leave the villa. Jude wondered if the man's fear had been realized upon his return to Rome's charge.

The heat of the day drove Jude from the upstairs meeting room down to the cool of the courtyard. There, he discovered a surprise.

"Joseph!" Jude rushed toward his brother. "When did you return?"

"Only moments ago," the older brother chuckled against the trappings of Jude's embrace.

"It's good to see you."

"And you." Joseph looked around. "Where is everyone else?"

"Some are upstairs enjoying a break from the heat of the day. Some have yet to return from their visits."

"Visits?"

"James' idea." Jude thumbed over his shoulder. "With the increase in Way Followers, Peter doubled our prayer times. We spend the first and ninth hour of almost every day at the Temple in prayer and sharing with those who come to Solomon's portico. Between those times, we are paired off and sent into the city to care for those in need. Mostly widows or injured men. Apart from our midday rest back here at the villa and Shabbat, we are either praying, teaching, or distributing food and supplies."

"Where does James get funds to be able to accomplish all this?"

"Adonai." Jude lifted his head. "Our God has pressed upon many to sell houses and lands and to bring the funds here. We've had more every day. Gracious givers have been showing up for days with money pouches full of coins and silver."

Joseph laughed. "It seems Adonai has been busy since I've been gone. I also seem to miss the most exciting times."

Jude lifted a shoulder. "There is plenty that still needs to be done. We receive news almost daily of another person in need."

"Jerusalem is a large city. I'm sure there are many in need within her walls."

Jude's thoughts shifted to his sister. "How is Assia?"

"I'm proud to report that she is happily married to her Hiskiel." He smirked.

"And our father's land?"

Joseph patted the money pouch tucked away in his tunic. "Sold."

A dark memory clouded Jude's mind as the image of Ananias and Sapphira laying on the floor colored his vision. "Be sure to get it to James."

Joseph raised a questioning eyebrow at his brother. "Why?"

"Just…" Jude hesitated to share about the two who had lied to Adonai and now lie in the sands of the Hinnom Valley. "Just make sure you get the pouch to James."

"Speaking of James." Joseph removed the sack from his back and placed it gently on the floor. "I have some of his tools from the house." He rummaged through the bag. "Some of yours as well."

Jude listened to the clang of wood, metal, and stone. He inwardly groaned at the physical reminders of his former trade. He'd give anything to never pick up another chisel for the rest of his days. His soul was much happier with the tools of his current trade, scrolls, his mind, and time to meditate.

"Here we are." Joseph lifted a wrapped set of chisels from his sack and handed them to Jude. "I will give James his when I bring him the funds."

Jude accepted his tools and leaned over the pack. "What else did you bring back?"

"Oh." Joseph pushed things around in the bag. "I found two tunics, Lydia's bronze mirror, Salome's

74

comb, a few odds and ends from the kitchen, and…" he carefully raised the next item, "…this."

With a gentle grasp, Jude took a worn sling from his brother's hand and held it up. "Is this Simon's?"

"I believe so." Joseph reached out for the weapon. "Assia and I found it. I thought I'd keep it." He held it close to his chest. "You know, for when he comes home."

Jude nodded in simple agreement. *If he comes home.*

Tucking the sling back into the sack, Joseph reached for the other set of tools and settled them in the crook of his arm. "Will you take the rest of this stuff to the girls? I guess I need to go find James."

"Sure." Jude tucked his wrapped tools in his armpit, picked up the pack, and headed for the kitchen.

The savory smells of the evening meal preparations greeted him. His stomach protested in response.

His mother smiled at him from her place near the fire. "What do you have there?"

Joseph moved deeper into the room and set the bag down on one of the tables along with his tools. "Joseph's back—"

"Joseph's back!" Mary clapped her hands. With a dash, she picked up the hem of her tunic and rushed from the room.

Jude stared after her before turning his gaze to Salome.

His youngest sister shook her head and lifted a shoulder. "What were you saying?"

"Joseph has returned from his trip." Jude dug around in the sack. "He brought some things from home." He lifted the bone comb. "He said this was yours."

Salome wiped her hands on a rag as she came closer. "It is." She plucked it from his hands. "Thank you."

"Lydia."

His middle sister looked up at him from her kneading.

"Joseph said this is yours." He raised the bronze mirror from the bag.

"It will be wonderful to have my own mirror again." She pushed the dough away from herself before pulling it back again. "You can leave it on the table. I'll retrieve it when my hands are free."

He set the polished, round metal on the table.

Salome mindlessly pressed her fingertips into the teeth of the comb. "Did Joseph bring anything else back?"

"Two tunics." He lifted one of the garments. "They look freshly washed. James' and my tools." His fingers grazed the sling. "Something for Simon." He looked up to catch a gentle gaze from Salome. "Some kitchen items." He returned his attention to the bag and placed the few bowls and knives on the table next to the mirror. "I guess he left some things with Assia."

"Oh, Assia," Salome squealed. "How is she? Does she enjoy being married? Did Joseph describe the wedding feast?"

Jude put his hands up and pushed the air in front of him. "Slow down."

She beamed at him with anticipation.

"All Joseph mentioned about Assia was that she was safely with Hiskiel's family. He didn't go into any more detail."

"Oh." She blew some stray hair away from her face. "Men never ask the right questions."

"I'm sure it was a lovely feast, and I'm sure Assia very much enjoys her husband."

"I do hope so." Salome brought her comb to her chest. "Just think. We might soon be dods and dodas."

The thought that his slightly older sister could, at this moment, be carrying a new life within her left a strange sensation in his body. He knew it was a great blessing to fill one's quiver with arrows to Adonai. He'd even entertained the thought of his own brood of young ones chasing each other around a home. With studying and his daily responsibilities, such ideas had been pushed to the back of his mind. Salome's eager optimism left him conflicted. He'd already lost the opportunity to enter into a betrothal agreement with two women. Would there ever be a woman to warm his sleeping mat on cold nights? Was there a woman in

Jerusalem who shared his passion for Adonai's Word and could still be a dutiful mother to children?

"It's so good to have Joseph back," Mary's voice returned Jude to the moment as she reentered the kitchen. She crossed the room to him and glanced at all the items on the table. "It seems as though he's brought back several things from the house."

Jude looked down to see the sling sitting in the pack.

"What have you got there?"

Jude brushed the braided rope. "It was Simon's." He looked up into his mother's face hoping not to see pain there. "Joseph brought it back for him."

"Well," she reached into the sack and retrieved the weapon, "we shall simply set it aside for him." She tucked the sling away into the folds of her tunic.

"Ima?"

Mary kept a faint smile on her face. "Hmm?"

"Do you worry about Simon?"

She nodded. "I try to leave all my children in Adonai's hands but that doesn't mean they are far from my mind. Besides," she wiped at her face, "it's not the first time I've lost a son to Jerusalem."

Jude chuckled at the recollection of Jesus' twelfth year in the city. The early memory of his parent's panic when they realized Jesus was not among the caravan heading back to Nazareth was as clear as any. "But Jesus was only lost for three days. Simon has been gone for months."

"And Adonai knew where Jesus was even when your father and I didn't, just like He knows where Simon is now. Even if we don't."

Jude marveled at her faith. Even when all hope seemed lost, his mother still held to her confidence in Adonai.

CHAPTER 12

After a night of fitful sleep, Jude broke his fast and reported to James for his assignment.

The past few days of service had left him feeling more like a soldier than a student. His time was mostly spent distributing food to those in need around the city. Peter's prayer times and James' distribution requirements left little of the day for Jude to study at the feet of his teacher. His eagerness to return to the scrolls chafed against his duty to his brother and Jesus' followers.

"Jude will be paired with John today," James' instructions interrupted Jude's thoughts.

Jude looked over at the younger man he'd spent much of his time trying to avoid.

One side of John's fuzzy lip rose in a half smile.

After the other pairs had been set and details given about where in the city their efforts would be focused for the day, James dismissed the gathering with prayer.

John moved with haste toward Jude. "I'm grateful for the opportunity to spend the day with you."

His youthful optimism made Jude feel older than he should have. "Let's get to the Temple. We don't want to be the last ones there."

The two traversed the city streets with ease behind the other disciples.

"James mentioned you are a student of Rabbi Ethan," John spoke with interest.

Jude cut his eyes at him. "And you are the son of a woman who is not your mother."

John flinched. "Your family is still sore about your brother's choice?"

It was Jude's turn to wince. "Jesus should have left her in the care of James."

"Perhaps his choice held more than just her care in mind."

"What do you mean?"

"If he had not given me such responsibility, I would not be who I am today." John turned toward the street leading to the Temple. "If James had maintained responsibility for Mary, you'd all be back in Nazareth by now. Think of all those who would still be in need if your family had not stayed in the city."

"There would still be Peter and the others."

"True." John laughed and playfully punched Jude's shoulder. "But we would be much less organized."

Jude allowed the silence to fill the space between them until they were closer to the Temple. But a question tugged at his troubled mind. He decided to seize the opportunity to have it answered. "How well do you know Peter?"

"My family has partnered with his for years. I know the man well enough, why?"

Jude adjusted the bag across his body which contained their portion of supplies they were to distribute. "Is he the common fisherman he claims or is there more to him?"

"I don't think I understand."

"The way he speaks. It's almost as if he's been a student all his life instead of spending his days on a boat in the Sea of Galilee."

John was deep in thought for several moments. "Answer me this, how did we speak in tongues we'd never been taught on Shavuot?"

"Adonai's Spirit."

John raised a knowing brow.

"You're saying the Spirit speaks through Peter?"

"I don't think Adonai always needs scholars and scribes. I believe He can use any mouth as long as the soul attached bends to Him."

Jude thought about John's words the rest of the way to the Temple. For one so young, Jude wondered how he and the other fishermen, those so common, spoke wisdom beyond their station. Of course, his brother had also been a common man.

The sun rose just as they arrived at Solomon's Colonnade. Incense poured up from the inner court and perfumed the air around Jude. Earthy scents of frankincense, galbanum, onycha, and myrrh mixed with sweeter notes of stacte and cassia and collided with the musk of spikenard. The special blend of seven spices could only be burned in the Temple and ascended upward twice a day. A column of smoke mimicked the one Adonai used to send down, though the glory cloud had been absent for decades.

Jude noticed people lined along the wall. "Who are they?" He pointed to the gathering.

"They are waiting for us," John answered.

"Why?"

"They've heard about what Peter did for the man who laid lame at the Beautiful Gate. They line up here for a chance to be healed too."

As they passed, people bowed their heads and pushed gifts toward their feet.

John stopped to accept their offerings.

Jude watched the other disciples gather around the porch for prayer.

Lastly, Peter passed by the line. When his shadow covered each person, they shouted praises to Adonai.

Jude couldn't believe his eyes. Lame people stood on healthy legs. Sick ones breathed fresh life into their bodies. Even those with unclean spirits calmed. "They are being healed from simply being in his shadow."

John rose to his feet with arms full. "'Then the eyes of the blind shall be opened, and the ears of the deaf unstopped. Then shall the lame man leap like a deer, and the tongue of the mute shall sing for joy.'"

The last line of his recitation struck Jude's soul. "W-w-what did you say?"

"It's from the prophet Isaiah. 'Then the eyes—'"

"The last part."

John thought for a moment. "'The tongue of the mute shall sing for joy.'"

Arava. Her form danced in his vision and her song of praise from his dream filled his thoughts. "John, we have a change of direction for the day."

John looked at him. "You know someone in need?"

"Yes." Jude watched people's faces flood with tears as they held their ears. "Someone in great need."

After psalms, prayers, and Peter's teaching about Jesus, the pairs were dismissed into the city.

With unsure steps, Jude led John toward the home of Chislon.

When they came upon the impressive structure, Jude's confidence bolstered. *Imitation marble.* He let the thought drift. *Only an experienced stoneworker could tell the difference.*

Even with the detail tucked away in his private thoughts, the knowledge that Chislon was a very important man in Jerusalem with a son rising in the ranks of the Council was not lost on Jude.

An ache to help a woman he barely knew pushed him toward the door. He called out, "Peace to this house."

A round woman with a grim countenance filled the

doorway. "Yes?"

Jude recognized her as Arava's mother, Batia, from the brief encounters he had with her and the rest of the family. "May I speak with…" His intentions clashed with sense for the first time. He couldn't ask for Arava. He had no way of communicating with her. Then an idea struck. "Talia."

Batia's eyes squinted with examination. "Talia has joined Raphu's family."

That's right. Jude's memory of the wedding feast came crashing back. His attempts to forget his previous interest in the eldest sister had served him well—until this moment. "Oh, may I speak with…" The names of the other sisters escaped him.

Batia's brows lowered with frustration.

"Ima?" a younger, female voice came from behind her. "Is everything well?"

Jude saw one of the sisters appear behind Batia and attempted to plead with her using only his eyes.

"This man is looking for Talia." Batia motioned toward Jude.

"Oh, Jude. Remember, Ima, we hosted them for an evening meal a while back." She nodded. "I can take him to see Talia."

Batia glanced from her daughter to the two men standing at her door. "Make it quick, Yana."

"Yes, Ima." Yana scooted around her mother like one moving around a hole in the ground. As she passed

Jude, she whispered, "Follow me."

Jude bowed toward Batia and motioned for John to follow them.

CHAPTER 13

The three walked several paces away from the house in silence.

John broke the peace first. "I thought we were visiting someone in need."

Yana paused. "Someone in need?"

Jude glanced over his shoulder to make sure Batia was not in listening range. The doorway of the home stood empty. "I'm sorry to visit unannounced. I came to see Arava."

"Arava?" Yana looked back at her home. "What do you want with my sister?"

"I want to help her." Jude tugged at the strap across his body. He knew nothing inside the bag would help Arava more than what awaited her in Peter's shadow.

"I'm afraid my father will not look kindly on your offer."

Jude studied her for a moment. "No." He realized his intentions had been misinterpreted. "I came to offer her something much better than a life alongside a simple craftsman."

"What then?"

"The chance for healing."

Yana searched him up and down. "Healing? No matter what herbs or balm are contained in your bag they will not work. My family doesn't believe in wasting money on false promises of healing from mixtures and flattering tongues."

"No." Jude rubbed his forehead. "I want to bring her to Peter. He has healed many in the name of my brother. I believe he can heal Arava just like the others. I simply need to take her to him."

Yana shook her head. "I'm afraid that won't be possible."

"Why not?"

She let out a heavy breath. "When Talia became part of Raphu's table, Arava lost her connection to the outside world. She's withdrawn. Without the watchful eyes of Talia, my Abba doesn't allow her to even leave the house."

John took a step toward her. "He keeps her prisoner?"

"For lack of a better explanation." Yana waved her hand as if to brush off his concern. "Zera and I try to communicate with her, try to help her, but she doesn't trust us as much as she did Talia."

Jude's frustration mounted. "Maybe if you explained our offer to her, she would agree to come with us."

"I wouldn't know how," Yana grunted. "Arava's been watching lips since she was a child but it's not an effective way to communicate with her. I only know some of her gestures."

"Talia." Jude attempted to keep his former interest from coloring her name. "If we can talk to Talia, I'm sure we can convince her to speak with Arava."

"I wouldn't count on that attempt." Yana stood firm. "Abba has been clear. Talia wouldn't do anything to cross him. Not even for Arava."

Jude's thoughts went to his own sister. "My sister communicates with her—the gestures—Salome picked up on them quickly."

"It wouldn't matter." Yana turned toward her home and hung her head. "Abba wants Arava to remain concealed for her protection. His will is final."

Jude watched her walk away while doubts about Arava's protection circled his thoughts. He was sure the act of hiding her away was more for the protection of Saul's reputation than for her wellbeing.

John lifted his palms toward Jude. "Now what?"

"Now we distribute our supplies." He adjusted the strap that hung heavily across his body.

"You are not going to let this matter go, are you?"

Jude turned to face John. "For one so young, you are very perceptive."

"For one so old, you should know better than to poke a sleeping viper."

Jude chuckled at the jest but the warning struck deep. He had no status compared to Saul's family.

They had loyal ties to Rome and more wealth than he would see in his lifetime. He was a simple man from a simple family and a simpler town in Galilee. If he continued to press into the affairs of a prominent family in Jerusalem, it could mean more trouble than he could handle.

"Let's get to our work." John headed in the direction of the Lower City they had been assigned.

Something held Jude to his spot. He glanced back toward the home of Chislon. Something moved on the roof. He squinted to get a better look but saw nothing else. The dream of Arava's praise tugged at him. *How can she praise You, Adonai, if You keep her ears blocked and her tongue still?*

"You coming?" John called to him.

With reluctant steps, Jude followed after him but kept his thoughts silent as they journeyed to the home of Sherra.

John paused at the door. "Peace to this house."

They both stepped back and waited.

Due to her advanced age and a bad hip, Sherra took a lot longer than most people to greet visitors. Eventually, she brought herself to the doorway. "Shalom."

"Shalom," the two men returned the greeting in unison.

"John," she reached out to pinch the younger man's cheek, "you grow more handsome every time I see you."

John's face reddened at the evaluation.

"How is Mary?"

"She is quite well." John puffed his chest. "She asks about you. She wants to make sure we are keeping an eye on you."

Sherra chuckled. "That woman worries for me as if I were one of her own when I'm old enough to be her mother." She turned her attention to Jude. "And who is this? He looks familiar."

"This is Jude ben Joseph." John waved to Jude. "He is one of Mary's sons."

A smile cracked Sherra's deep wrinkles. "You look a lot like your brother, Joseph."

"I get that often." Jude reached into his sack and brought forth a wrapped loaf of bread and a small bag of dried fruit. "These are from my mother and the other followers. Know they also accompany our prayers for you."

"I will receive both with many thanks." She held out shaking hands to accept the offerings.

"Are you well?" John asked. "Anything that needs doing around here?"

Jude let his gaze take in the widow's home. It was a simple structure but appeared well looked after.

Sherra glanced up. "The roof might need tending before the colder weather comes in."

John nodded with her assessment. "We can get a

few of us up there with some patches and fresh branches." He let his gaze fall back down to her. "Anything else?"

"How is my neighbor?"

John looked at Jude.

"She means Salvus," Jude offered. "We were able to break his fever. His wound had begun to heal but he left without allowing it to fully heal."

She fixed her eyes intently on Jude. "You let him leave?"

"I had no choice in the matter. I begged him to stay." Jude shook his head. "There was no persuading him. He wanted to report to his commander as soon as he could walk."

Sherra glanced up and down the dusty road. "I haven't seen him."

"He reported to the Fortress," Jude explained. "He was only staying in the city temporarily while the influx of other soldiers occupied space in the Fortress for Passover and Herod's visit."

"I see." She leaned heavily on her staff. "Have you no word?"

"None." Jude looked at his sandals. "I've thought many times about seeking him out in the Fortress but it seems like a fruitless endeavor."

"Well," she tapped her staff, causing dust to stir, "I shall continue to pray for him and we will leave him in the hands of Adonai."

John bowed to Sherra. "If you'll excuse us, we have others we need to visit before the hour of prayer."

Jude glanced up into the sky and found the sun further along than he had planned. "Yes, and we must be quick about it. James doesn't like it when we're late."

CHAPTER 14

After emptying the sack into the hands of other needy widows, Jude led John back to the Temple. The courts bustled with an abundance of people coming to seek Temple services.

Jude entered Solomon's Colonnade under the firm gaze of James. Try as they did to avoid it, he and John had been the last of the followers to arrive. The group was waiting for them. They took their typical place among the others and joined in the hour of prayer.

After reciting a praise song of David, Peter taught with his usual authority as the crowd around them grew larger.

The press of people made Jude uncomfortable. It was difficult to blend into the daily gathering of worshipers when curious crowds filled the porch to hear of Jesus or wait for an opportunity to be healed.

"I don't like this." His voice was low against the boldness of Peter's.

John caught his attention and lifted a shoulder.

"We should be much more careful."

"It's been months since Jesus was crucified." John leaned closer to be heard. "We shouldn't have to keep hiding."

"Peter has already been warned by the Council." He pointed his finger at John's chest. "You've been personally charged not to speak my brother's name in public as well. Do you want to end up back in a cell?"

John puffed his thin chest against Jude's finger. "I did wear chains for Messiah, and I would gladly do so again."

"We will be no help to anyone if we are rotting in a—" Jude's argument was cut off by the horrid sight of High Priest Caiaphas and a group of Sadducees storming their direction. "Oh no."

The gathering split like the Red Sea their ancestors crossed with Moses. People dashed in different directions as the arrogant leaders set their steps toward Peter and the other disciples.

John crouched as if he were going to run toward the religious leaders.

Jude grabbed his tunic and pulled the younger man back. "Get to the villa!" He screamed over the chaos. "This is no time to pick another fight with Caiaphas."

John tugged out of his grasp and ran straight at one of the Sadducees who had hold of Peter.

On raised toes, Jude searched for James and Joseph. In the confusion, he couldn't tell where they were. He decided going back to the villa was the safest option.

As he turned to leave, he ran straight into the breastplate of Uzzi, the captain of the Temple guard.

The unusually tall Hebrew gripped the back of Jude's arm to hold him in place. "Where do you think you're running off to?"

Jude thrashed against his hold without answering the question.

"You're coming with me, Galilean."

Jude struggled to free himself as he was dragged closer to the others who were already bound. He didn't see James or Joseph. Inward relief clashed with a sickening feeling in the pit of his stomach that he would share in enduring whatever fate awaited his brother's followers. The sensation intensified when he caught the uneven grin of John.

"Get ties on this one, too." Uzzi shoved Jude toward a guard.

He tumbled forward, landing in the open arms of the man.

The guard wrapped a thick rope around his wrists and jerked to pull his hands together before securing the binding with an expert knot.

Jude felt the rub of the constricting cord dig into his flesh.

With a longer line, Uzzi joined the men together in a humiliating display.

Jude felt like an exile being led away from home into foreign territory.

John glanced over his shoulder at him. "Looks like we get to share a cell this time."

He groaned as he glared up at the pinnacles of the Fortress of Antonia which poked against the sky.

As Uzzi led them underground to the public prison Jude remembered Salvus' warning. If Rome held their bindings, their fate would be much worse. Since they had been arrested by the Temple guard, they would be held in a cell under the Temple until a formal council could gather the following morning to decide their fate.

As they descended several levels of stairs in silence, Jude's nose twitched at the stench which permeated the air. The smell reminded him of the market—animals mixed with people. Yet, instead of life scents, this place smelled of death and decay.

At the bottom, Uzzi moved toward a large door. He used a key to unlock the heavy barrier and pulled it open. "In here." He pointed.

Another guard pushed the line forward from behind. "Move it!"

As the disciples walked toward the opening, Uzzi untied each man's hands. When they had all piled into the dark room, he closed the door.

Jude's heart sank as the lock clicked behind him. His knees shook in the darkness and he feared falling on them without knowing what lay under his feet.

He stood still for several moments allowing his eyes to adjust to the lack of light. Something moved beside him and he jumped.

"Better get some sleep."

Jude recognized Peter's voice but couldn't yet make out his full form.

"Morning will come."

An inner groan filled Jude. How was he going to be able to sleep in a crowded cell? He didn't know what awaited him with the sunrise.

Something scurried around his feet, and he heard both the sound of tiny nails on stone and the high-pitched squeal of vermin.

Jude's skin crawled. Even in the depths of his poverty, he'd never slept with rats. He was unsure if sleep would be a welcomed relief or provide himself as a meal for the pests that infested the common prison.

A hand touched his shoulder.

He spun around.

"Peace."

"J-John?" Jude's voice quaked.

"You should really get some sleep. There isn't anything else you can do. I can push some of the straw against the wall for you."

Jude heard the rustling of straw and he held out his hands in an attempt to discover his temporary bedding. His fingers bumped into something hard and cold; what he assumed was a wall.

"Here."

He felt John's grasp on his wrist.

John pulled him down and put his hand on top of

the pile of straw.

Jude lowered himself. "Thanks." He put his back against the wall and adjusted on the prickly material. Once seated, he did his best to settle himself.

"I wonder if it was like this for your mother."

John's statement burned in Jude's heart. He was both confused by it and saddened at what his mother would feel once the others told her of his fate. "Ima. My poor mother ."

"I wouldn't worry too much about her." John chuckled. "It's not like she hasn't had a son in chains before."

Jealousy and anger boiled with frustration in him. "You're not really her son."

"I meant Jesus."

Jude's eyes adjusted enough to see John within a hand's width of him. The young man held hurt clear on his unwrinkled face. "I'm sorry."

"Your first time can be frightening."

First time. Jude thought about the implication. If he had anything to do with it, this would be his first and only time in a cell. He decided to change the flow of the conversation. "What did you mean about Ima?"

"Oh," John picked up a piece of straw and tucked one end of it into his mouth, "the story she shared about the night Jesus was born. Having to give birth with the livestock because the inn was so crowded." He glanced around. "I imagine it must have felt kind of like this."

"Which one of us is the donkey?" Philip joked.

Uneasy laughter spread around the room.

Jude simply shook his head.

"I'd rather be a sheep," Peter called from the other side of the room.

"I'd rather get some sleep," Thomas countered.

"Thomas is right," Peter admitted. "We could all use a good night's sleep to prepare for tomorrow."

Jude doubted this night's sleep could ever be counted as good.

He bowed his head in the darkness and prayed his customary evening prayer, *Adonai, may it be Your will that I lie down in peace and rise up in peace.* He nearly scoffed at the irony. *Let not my thoughts or my dreams disturb me. Watch over my family and those I love.* His thoughts momentarily returned to his mother and his sisters. They must be worried sick over his absence.

O Guardian of Israel, who neither slumbers nor sleeps, I entrust my spirit to You. Thus, as I go to sleep, I put myself into Your safekeeping. Grant me a night of rest. He opened his eyes to take in the cell he shared with the others. His body echoed the plea.

Let the healing processes that You have placed into my body go about their work. May I awaken in the morning, refreshed, and renewed to face a new tomorrow.

His gaze graced the low ceiling knowing that

somewhere above him stood the Temple. *Hear, O Israel, Adonai our God, Adonai is One! We praise You, Adonai, Whose shelter of peace is spread over us, over all Your people Israel, over every creation, and over Jerusalem.*

CHAPTER 15

Light pierced Jude's closed eyelids. Sometime in the night he had huddled into the straw and fallen asleep. Without knowing how long he'd slumbered, he lifted a hand to block the blinding illumination. "What is that? It can't be day."

"Peace."

A voice so powerful and bold shook Jude like a quake. He tried to peer through his fingers to see into the brightness but it was too much. Fearing he was dreaming, he looked around.

The twelve other men in the room all stared in disbelief at the brilliant form standing in the room with them.

For the first time since entering the cell, Jude could see the faces of every one of his brother's followers. They all appeared as white as a sailing sheet. Their eyes were as large and dark as onyx stones.

Peter rose and faced the light. "What do you want with us?"

"Go."

Jude saw what appeared to be a hand from the brightness point toward the door.

"Stand in the Temple and speak to the people all the words of this Life."

The next sound Jude heard was the lock clicking open and the groan of the hinges of the heavy door swinging wide. He couldn't believe the sight. He knew it had to be a dream.

The form of light moved through the door and toward the stairs.

Peter hurried after it without discussion.

Most of the others followed with haste.

John stood up.

With shaking legs, Jude rose as well. "Tell me you saw it, too."

"Of course." The younger man smiled. "It's a messenger." He passed through the door.

"Messenger." He'd only seen the two messengers that had told them to wait for Jesus' return by the Mount of Olives and heard of the ones that had visited his parents. This one shone so brightly in the darkness of the cell, he had not been able to make out much of its form.

Jude peered out of the cell expecting to see two guards waiting at the door to escort them back into the cell. Yet, the main room was empty. "Odd." Without another moment of hesitation, he rushed toward the steps.

As he ascended the steps, he watched John take them two at a time to surpass the older men. Jude came upon Andrew at the end of the group. "Tell me I'm not dreaming."

"If you are, we are all sharing in it." The fisherman pressed upward.

Jude kept behind the others as they passed the lower levels of the underground storage areas and came up to the Temple courtyard.

It was quiet for a moment as Jude reached the last step. The messenger was gone. Night faded around them in the empty courtyard. A moment later, Jude looked up to see incense smoke billow above them as the first rays of sunlight shone on the white marble of Herod's Temple. The signal for day.

Peter waved to the group. "Come." He led them to Solomon's Colonnade where they had gathered twice a day for weeks.

As soon as Jude saw Peter's intention, he rushed to confront him. "What are you doing?"

"Obeying the messenger."

Jude looked around. "We were in that cell for this and you want to go right back to it?"

Peter put a firm hand on Jude's shoulder. "We need to obey and leave the results with Adonai."

The skin-crawling memory of rats, darkness, and a cramped cell flooded Jude.

"Look at me," Peter commanded.

Jude fixed his gaze on the older man.

"Obey and leave the results with Adonai." He

squeezed his shoulder for emphasis.

The messenger's charge to speak overshadowed his fear. He nodded.

A small crowd formed around them under the shade of the porch.

As Peter began to teach, the others joined in sharing about Jesus with anyone who would stop long enough to listen.

Jude was sharing with a man when he saw Uzzi and his officers heading in their direction. He turned toward Peter and pointed. "We are about to have company."

Peter stood firm as the Temple guards made their way to them.

Uzzi spread his arms wide. "What is the meaning of this display?"

Peter stared him down in a silent challenge.

"The council has assembled. I went to bring you to them. I discovered my guards still standing watch and the door securely locked, but your cell was empty."

Jude looked at Peter, but the old fisherman stood as tall as a Roman statue.

"You all need to come with me. Now."

The group of men waited for Peter to move.

Jude glanced at the crowd gathered around them. This time they had not fled in fear. They stood by waiting to see what would become of the men who followed Jesus. He noticed Uzzi hesitate as his gaze brushed the growing throng, too.

"Come freely, and I won't have to use force," Uzzi hissed between his teeth.

Peter nodded and stepped forward.

The guard led them to the Chamber of Hewn Stone.

Jude's throat tightened as they entered the semi-circled room filled with Pharisees, Sadducees, the High Priest's family members, and other distinguished men of Israel. For so much of his life, he longed to sit among them as an equal. This morning, he stood before them as a prisoner. He hung his head in shame.

Caiaphas sat in the center chair at the head of the room. "We strictly charged you not to teach in this name, yet here you have filled Jerusalem with your teaching, and you intend to bring this man's blood upon us. You are in direct violation of our order."

Jude noticed Caiaphas choosing his words carefully and that his brother's name was not found on his lips.

Standing in front of the rest, Peter spoke for the others, "We must obey Adonai rather than men. The God of our fathers raised Jesus, whom you killed by hanging him on a tree." He raised his right hand to the ceiling. "Adonai exalted him at His right hand as Leader and Savior, to give repentance to Israel and forgiveness of sins. We are witnesses to these things," he let his hand drop to his chest, "and so is the Holy Spirit, whom Adonai has given to those who obey

Him."

Jude watched red creep up Caiaphas' neck from under his collar and reached up to his ears. "Perhaps we should stone you for such blasphemy. Then your tongues might cease their lies."

"Caiaphas."

Jude turned toward the voice. He recognized it immediately. Gamaliel, his most sought-after Rabbi, stood among the Pharisees.

"I have something to say."

Caiaphas waved toward him. "Speak on."

"Men of Israel," Gamaliel paused to make sure he had the attention of everyone in the room, "take care what you are about to do with these men. Before these days, Theudas rose up, claiming to be somebody, and a number of men, about four hundred, joined him. He was killed, and all who followed him were dispersed and came to nothing.

"After him, Judas, the Galilean, rose up in the days of the census and drew away some of the people after him. He too perished, and all who followed him were scattered. So, in this present case, I tell you, keep away from these men and let them alone. If this plan or this undertaking is of man, it will fail; but if it is of Adonai, you will not be able to overthrow them." He set his ancient gaze on Jude. "You might even be found opposing Adonai!"

Jude attempted to hide his eyes from the teacher

by moving behind John.

Gamaliel sat back down.

Jude's attention flicked to the High Priest.

Caiaphas templed his fingers on his lips. "The Pharisee speaks with much wisdom."

A flicker of hope rose in Jude. He'd have to think of a way to thank the Rabbi for his words on their behalf. Though he was sure his wisdom came from not wanting to share in more bloodshed and less from his approval of their actions.

"Let us make our order clearer." Caiaphas leveled his gaze at Peter. "Beat them."

"No!" Jude screamed as one of the guards grabbed his arm.

CHAPTER 16

Jude thrashed against the guard's grip.

Uzzi moved in front of him and grabbed Jude's jaw with one hand forcing him to match his gaze. "This one has enough fire for the full amount. Remove his tunic."

The guard ripped Jude's belt from his waist and tossed it to the ground. Without care, he forced the outer tunic over Jude's head, exposing a single woven undergarment for all to see.

Jude's stomach turned remembering Ethan's description of Roman soldiers casting lots for Jesus' clothing as he hung on their torture display. His precious mother's fingerprints interlaced with every strand of the simple garments she had made for each of her children.

Reaching out, the guard gripped the cord around Jude, pulled it, and threw it onto the growing pile of clothes. He set his other hand on the top opening of the material.

Not wanting his undergarment to be torn, Jude shrugged out of the short tunic before the guard could rip it from him. The chill of morning air caressed

Jude's exposed skin causing him to shudder. At that moment, the full weight of humiliation crashed on him. He wished he'd chosen to follow the ways of the Essenes like his cousin John so that he would at least have a loincloth to cover his shame. He'd never been this bare before anyone in his adult life. His indignity was on display for those he'd hoped to expose his mind. Nothing he could ever do would rub out this moment from their memories.

The guard put a warm hand on Jude's bare shoulder and shoved him to the ground.

Pain shot up Jude's thighs as his knees crashed into the hard marble. The cool stone, not yet heated by the warmth of the day, sent a shiver up his back.

Uzzi stood over him with his hand held open.

Another guard walked over and placed a whip into his palm.

The captain closed his hand around the three strains of calfskin, each one as thick as a man's finger. He gripped the handle with his free hand and pulled the cords through his fingers as a smirk lifted the corners of his lips.

Jude looked up into Peter's eyes. The older man's command echoed in his mind. *Obey and leave the results with Adonai.*

With heavy steps, Uzzi moved behind Jude.

Preparing for the first wave of lashes, Jude hunched and closed his eyes.

As the whip hit his bare skin, it brought with it pain unlike anything he'd ever endured and a cracking sound mimicking the break of a bone.

A guard counted off, "One."

Another wave hit as tears stung his eyes.

"Two."

The snap of leather across his back struck again.

"Three."

With each blow, he was grateful that the whip contained three cords, each counted as a lash. He'd only need to endure thirteen strikes in accordance with Moses' restriction. *Mercy*. He thought with the next lash. *Even in the midst of judgment, Adonai shows mercy.*

"Four."

Jude bent further forward as burning spread across his back.

"Five."

With the next lash, something on his back felt as if it tore. Jude imagined his skin ripping open.

"Six."

His lungs burned with another hit.

"Seven."

His knees ached under his weight and bent position.

"Eight."

The hits came in rhythmic timing.

"Nine."

He dug his fingernails into the marble.

"Ten."

Jude saw droplets of blood hit the ground beside him.

Caiaphas' hand rose from the arm of the ornate chair.

Uzzi stood over Jude and yanked his head upward by his hair.

Jude panted like a deer waiting for the relief of a hunter's knife after a misplaced arrow.

The captain dropped his hold on Jude's head. "He can still endure."

Caiaphas waved him on and leaned back in his seat.

Another blow struck across Jude's bleeding back.

"Eleven."

Pain and burning reached down into his arms.

"Twelve."

Red filled his vision.

"Thirteen."

As Caiaphas' hand came up again, Jude crumbled forward. He wheezed against the cold stone. The ornate patterns held no beauty at that moment. Instead, they mocked him with their lack of warmth and comfort.

Uzzi nudged him to his side with his foot. "Get the next one ready."

Guards grabbed Jude by his arms and hauled him out of the way.

His head swam as his face skidded across the marble.

When he was clear, they released their hold on his arms.

The thud of his hands hitting the ground brought a roll of sickness to Jude's stomach. He attempted to press himself up but the motion brought on another wave of nausea. The cool touch of the stone against his bare skin made him tremble.

When he was finally able to lift his gaze, he saw John remove his tunics and kneel in front of Uzzi. Everything in him ached to throw himself over the young man. He lurched forward only to meet the marble with the side of his face as his vision dimmed.

Laying on the floor of the Chamber of Hewn Stone, Jude watched the twelve men who had put their lives in his brother's hands take their thirty-nine lashes for teaching that Jesus is Messiah.

Is this what you endured, brother? He cried out in the quiet of his mind. *Is this what you had in mind for us?*

By the time the final disciple had received his punishment, Jude was able to sit upright. He clawed at his clothes and shoved his tunics back over his body. The touch of the material against his open back felt like rubbing salt in the wounds. He swayed on weak legs as he stood with the others before Caiaphas.

"Do not speak or teach in the name of Jesus ever

again." The High Priest expressed every word as if each stood as a command of its own. "Go." He brushed them off as if they were pests invading his peace.

The group departed the chamber and went into the courtyard.

Out in the open, Peter hit his knees with his hands lifted toward the inner courtyard. "Praise You, Adonai, that you have counted us worthy to suffer dishonor for the name of Your Messiah."

John and the others joined him in praise.

Jude stood staring at them. After what they had endured, he felt ready to pack his things and leave Jerusalem and his brother's teachings far behind. His spirit had borne an equal lashing to his skin.

As he looked up toward the golden spikes protruding from the top of the holiest of holies giving an appearance of a crown, he thought about the crown of thorns his brother wore. He considered the Roman scourging Jesus had suffered. An event monumentally worse than what he had just experienced due to Rome's unique bend toward extracting every measure of torture during their punishments. He counted the hours Jesus hung pierced to a wooden cross and the mocking shame of his fellow Hebrews mixed with physical humiliation.

Tears streamed down Jude's face as he realized each agonizing moment of that day Jesus was declaring his love for all people by paying the way back to Adonai with his blood. He realized that getting to know the truth about Messiah was more than a mental exercise among scrolls. Jesus had suffered for all; surely he could suffer for the One.

His knees buckled under the weight of such comprehension. "Praise You, Adonai. You have counted me worthy to suffer for Jesus, Your Messiah."

CHAPTER 17

The journey back to the villa was filled with more praises from the lips of those whose backs bled for sharing truth. Jude joined in psalm after psalm the men chanted as they marched toward their dwelling.

They entered the priest's home with shouts of praise so loud that the commotion brought the servants and other residents from their tasks.

Mary rushed toward the group of men. "We've been worried sick." She examined them. "What happened to you?"

John turned around to expose his bloody tunic. "We bear the stripes of Jesus."

Mary gasped at the sight. She put her hands on his back. "Salome! Lydia! Fresh linens!" She looked over to Jude. "You as well?"

He slowly turned around.

She inhaled a quick breath through closed teeth.

Jude looked over his shoulder in an attempt to see how large the stain had spread. "That bad?"

"You will all need tending." She pulled her hands away from John's back. "Go upstairs."

The men ascended the steps as obedient sons and

settled in the upper room they often used for meetings and prayer. There they removed their soiled garments and wrapped linens around their waists.

Mary returned with her two daughters, the two female servants, and enough supplies to tend the wounds. The women worked to clean each stripe with gentle care before wrapping the men's backs and providing clean tunics.

Salome moved to Jude.

He lay on his stomach so she could more easily clean and rinse his open wounds.

She worked in silence.

After a few moments, he looked up and noticed a single tear running down her cheek. "Do you weep for me, sister?"

She wiped the dampness away with the back of her hand. "I was just wondering how many of my brothers would have to endure such treatment."

Jude turned his gaze forward. "We suffer because he suffered."

"I know." She lifted a jar. "We don't have much of this balm left."

Jude looked around. "Who else needs care?"

"Just John."

"Save it for him."

Salome hesitated. "Your wounds are deep. The balm will help keep away infections."

"Do as I ask." He glanced over at the younger man.

"I will heal."

She set down the jar and worked to bind his wounds. "I guess your view of him has changed."

Jude glanced over at John once more. "My view on a lot has changed."

The servants gathered the bloody garments and left to scrub them before the stains set in.

Jude slipped an older undergarment over the cloth around his waist before removing it and then lowered a clean outer tunic over himself. His movements were impeded by his freshly bound back. "Where are James and Joseph?"

Salome gathered the linens. "They left early this morning to make visits and had plans to go to the Temple to hear of your fate." She twisted a cloth in her hand. "They told us what happened when they returned yesterday."

"Sherra." Jude's memory returned. "She needs us to inspect her roof before the change in season."

"I'll let James know when they get back." She slowly lifted her gaze. "What happened to you?"

He turned to meet the glistening eyes of his mother. "Are you sure you two want to hear this story?"

Both women nodded in unison.

Jude recounted the previous day's events starting with the widows. He intentionally left out his trip to Chislon's home until he could speak with Salome alone. He spoke of the crowds and the guards and the night locked in the cell.

"That must have been awful." Salome shook her head.

"It was." Jude remembered the scurrying of rats and fought to keep from shivering. "But in the middle of the night, a messenger freed us."

"You mean someone sent from the council?"

"Someone sent from Adonai. They told us to go back to the courtyard and continue teaching about Jesus." He spread out his palms. "So, we did. But the guards found us there and took us before the council. Because we had defied their previous orders, they beat us." He massaged his aching shoulder. "Then they let us go but not before reminding us of their command. We are not to teach about Jesus."

Salome huffed. "Those arrogant men should find better things to do than beat people who speak truth."

Lydia put her hands on her hips. "You're not going back to teach in the Temple anymore, right?"

"Of course they are," Salome answered before Jude had a chance. "Jesus told them to and so did a messenger. You think Caiaphas has more authority than they?"

"He's the High Priest."

"He's a pious peacock hiding behind the colorful stones of our ancestors."

Jude couldn't help the chuckle that escaped at his

feisty youngest sister. He looked at his mother. "Ima, I think I finally understand why you left us to follow Jesus."

She let her head dip to one side.

"I didn't understand. Not at first." He put his hand on the back of his neck and lifted a shoulder. "I didn't understand why you left us for him. We thought he was a lunatic, and you were simply chasing after a wayward son." He dropped his arm. "I think I get it now. You followed because Jesus is Messiah. To follow him, one must give up their own life and walk in his steps. It's kind of like being a student to a Rabbi. You have to let go of what you know in order to become like your teacher."

Mary smiled. "Your brother shared a similar lesson with a man who came seeking him for the path to eternal life."

"Will you share the lesson with me?"

"I remember the man was very proud that he had been able to keep every command from his youth." Her eyes drifted away with the recollection of the memory. "Jesus said there was only one thing he lacked."

"What?"

"To take all of his wealth and give it to the poor and then he could follow."

"Did he?"

"He was quite distraught over the request. He had

spent his lifetime accumulating his treasures." Mary shook her head. "We never saw him again." She waved to the other men in the room. "Jesus told his disciples that it was difficult for those with wealth to enter the kingdom of Adonai. That it was easier for a camel to pass through the eye of the needle than it was for a rich person to enter the kingdom."

Jude rubbed his bearded chin. "Like the eye of the needle gate here in Jerusalem and the one back in Nazareth?"

"Exactly." Mary put up a finger. "How would you get a camel through one of those gates?"

"The walking gate is built narrow and low to keep enemies out." His mind turned over the parable. "A camel ladened with a heavy load for a long journey could not pass through it. One would have to unload the animal and have him bow to enter."

"That's what Jesus was trying to teach the wealthy man." Her face brightened. "It would be impossible for him to enter the narrow gate into the kingdom with the weight he carried. He would need to untangle himself from the burden his treasures had on his soul and humble himself."

"Leaving behind the load."

"You understood faster than his followers." Mary set soft eyes on the men. "They asked for Jesus to clarify." She turned back to Jude. "He told them there was no one who had left house or brothers or sisters or mother or father or children or lands, for his sake who would not receive a hundredfold in this time, houses and brothers and sisters and mothers and children and lands, with persecutions, and eternal life in the age to come."

The disciples humbly nodded in agreement.

Jude held his mother's gaze. "We were your load."

She put her hand against his cheek. "You were the treasure I had spent a lifetime storing up. Each child more precious to me than silver or jewels. But when Jesus called me to follow, I had to lay aside those treasures to obey." She rubbed her fingers through the coarse hair of his beard. "I knew you would be called when the time came. I also knew that no matter what happened, I could never lose my treasures. Even if I laid them aside for a time."

John walked up and put an arm over her shoulder. "And Jesus fulfilled his promise by giving you twelve more sons."

Mary beamed at those standing around him. "And so many more."

Jude understood what his brother had been trying to teach the wealthy man. Letting go didn't mean losing; it meant being open for more gain. He had carried the load of achieving status among the religious leaders for so long. A load he needed to set down and humble himself. Glancing around the room, he realized he'd been given everything he needed.

"Ima, will you share more of what you remember of Jesus' teachings?"

Her smile widened.

"I want to know Him more."

CHAPTER 18

Jude attempted to stretch his aching back but the bruised muscles resisted. It had been weeks since his beating at the hands of Uzzi. Elissa had insisted Naomi be called to inspect each man's wounds for infection. The midwife then made a habit of examining them every few days and adjusting treatments as needed.

Jude's wounds were of the last to heal due to his repeated refusal of her balms and oils. He knew resources were scarce. It wasn't until the others' needs diminished that he finally gave in to the older woman's demands of treatment.

His wounds had finally healed to the point they no longer required binding but most movements brought a reminder of Caiaphas' order. An order Jude and the others had disobeyed on countless occasions. They still spoke in the Temple but also started meeting in homes. The choice was not out of fear but protection for those who would also endure the wrath of the council if they were caught.

Jude considered again the scroll he had selected for the day's study. "'...but bruises and sores and raw wounds; they are not pressed out or bound up or softened with oil.'" He nearly chuckled at Isaiah's symbolic description of wayward Israel. "Oh, prophet, if you only knew."

Ethan passed by the stone table. "Enjoying your meditations?"

"I don't find much difference in the leaders of Isaiah's day and ours. They are like shepherds feeding only themselves. Even to the disadvantage of their flocks."

Ethan's raised silver brow was an open invitation for his student to continue.

"Isaiah speaks not only against the people for their unfaithfulness but also against those in rule over them for not faithfully guiding them to Adonai." He let out a heavy sigh. "We have many in leadership today who are following the same path."

"Your soul still wrestles with Saul?"

Jude nodded. The man had been a repeated topic of discussion between Rabbi and student. "How can a person have such a reputation of righteousness without a measure of righteousness?"

"Saul is a Roman citizen because of where he was born. He learned at a young age how to use that advantage for personal gain." Ethan moved around the table toward Jude. "There will always be those who seek what they can gain from this life. And there will always be false teachers." He held up an open hand. "Does this mean we should tremble before them? Does this mean we should hide or stop speaking truth?"

He hung his head. "No."

"We cannot control the actions of others. We are called to walk our own path. One of truth."

Jude agreed with his teacher's assessments but the thought of Arava being trapped within the walls of false virtue still dug at him. "Maybe you're right."

Ethan layered his hands behind his back. "I think that's enough for today."

Jude looked up at him in disappointment.

"You're still healing and besides," he turned toward the doorway, "it's such a nice day. We should enjoy it before the colder weather comes upon us."

Jude wanted to argue but the ache in his back agreed with his Rabbi. He still needed time to recover.

The silent walk back to the villa gave him an opportunity to reflect not only on the prophet's words but his Rabbi's. He knew he should push Saul and his family from his mind but, try as he might, Arava had a hold on him he couldn't explain. Even though he'd not tried again to visit her, she often visited his dreams.

Once inside the safety of the villa, Jude sought out James. His mind was firm on two desires.

His older brother was with some of the disciples enjoying a rest from the middle of the day.

Jude reclined next to his brother and picked at the fruit and bread spread on the low table. "I've been considering something."

James plucked a grape from its vine. "When do you do anything else?" He tossed the fruit into his mouth.

"Something more specific," Jude defended. "Mostly about when I was held in the prison."

Darkness washed over James' face.

Jude noticed the dramatic shift in his brother's mood. He'd not spoken openly with James about his time in the custody of the Temple guard. Jude was not ashamed but he'd seen the brokenness it had caused James. The older brother acted as if he was responsible for every step their family took. Jude didn't wish to remind him of his seeming failure to protect another sibling from shackles. He hurried to explain his reason for raising the topic. "I was thinking about others who are locked away, especially those being held in Roman cells."

James held his peace but his countenance still held a shadow.

"I think they would benefit from our aid as the widows do. They hunger too. I'm sure many are in need of medical supplies to tend their wounds." Jude swallowed hard. "I think we should visit them."

James sat upright. "You know to visit such would be as if you bore their chains?"

"I've already endured the whips of the council." He lifted his head. "I have already shared in their shame."

"Very well." James brushed his hands together. "If you deem it a worthy cause, we shall see about including prisoners in our visits."

Jude grinned.

"But not the women," James clarified. "I don't want them anywhere near either of those places. Only the men will be permitted to make these visits."

Jude nodded ferociously in agreement. "Of course."

With one difficult conversation behind him, Jude retreated to the kitchen in search of someone who might offer him aid with another matter. "Sister?"

Salome stirred a stew over the cooking fire. "Brother?" she smirked with amusement.

He came closer as embarrassment sent warmth up the sides of his neck. "I've been considering something that I need your help with."

She straightened her back. "Speak on."

"Arava," he let the woman's name drop from his mouth like a heavy weight. "I want to ask her if she will come here to meet with Peter."

Realization brightened Salome's countenance in a single moment. "Healing. You want to see if Peter can heal her?"

Jude nodded slowly. "I tried to visit her home but I didn't get very far. I thought if I brought you, the two of us might have a better chance since you can communicate with her."

"Why didn't I think of that?" Salome smacked her forehead with the palm of her hand. "Of course Peter could heal her. He's helped so many."

Jude's shoulders lifted with hope. "So, you'll help?"

Salome held her tongue for a moment as a smile crept across her face.

"What?"

"Oh, nothing."

"Salome, I know that look."

She chuckled. "The truth always has a way of seeing the light of day."

Jude recognized the words of their older sister, Assia. The advice hit with force. He knew it to be true. It had always held true. If he did have feelings for Arava, they would be revealed at some point. He only hoped he could provide her some relief from the chains which held her captive regardless of their paths. She may not reside in a prison cell like those he hoped to aid, but she wasn't free either, and she could certainly benefit from being healed of her infirmities.

Salome held the stirring spoon to her chest. "When do we leave?"

Jude glanced around the room. "How soon can you get someone to take over the evening meal preparations?"

CHAPTER 19

Jude had to force his steps to slow so Salome could keep up with his hurried pace. He was nervous but also excited to see Peter perform a great act of healing in Arava's life. If she could hear and speak, her family would not feel the need to hide her away. She would be allowed to live; to be free. Who knows what else Adonai had planned for her with a voice and open ears?

As Chislon's moderate home came into view, Jude's heart picked up its pace. He moved toward the door and called, "Peace to this house."

Yana filled the frame. Her countenance was less than enthusiastic to see Jude.

"Shalom, Yana," Salome spoke behind her brother.

The woman peered around Jude to see her. "Shalom." She met eyes with Jude. "To what do we owe the honor?"

Jude caught the intended cynicism dripping from her pleasantries but didn't allow it to affect his aim. "We wish to visit Arava. You mentioned her withdrawal since your sister's wedding. I brought my sister in the hopes of cheering her up."

Yana searched Jude up and down before moving on

to Salome to do the same. "I don't know if my sister wants to see you."

Jude took a step closer. "Will you at least ask her?"

Yana's eyes squinted into measuring slits. She huffed and turned back into the home.

With a half turn over his shoulder, he whispered, "Do you think she'll ask?"

"I'm sure she'll try."

Jude righted himself and stared into the dim of the house. He wanted to exhaust every possible path to bring Arava to Peter. Even if he had to drag one to see the other, he'd at least give this woman an opportunity. Perhaps then she'd relinquish his dreams back to him.

After some time, Yana returned. She silently stood in the doorway.

Jude counted his heartbeats as the woman simply stared at them. "What did Arava say?"

"I tried my best but I don't think she understood me."

"Let us enter." Jude stepped forward. "Salome can communicate with her."

Yana's gaze laid down a challenge. "If my parents find out you were here or if Arava brings any trouble, I will adamantly deny I allowed you to enter this house. Whatever results of your visit, will not be laid at my feet. Is that clear?"

Jude violently nodded his head.

Yana glanced around him at Salome.

The younger woman bowed her head.

With a step to the side, Yana allowed them passage inside.

Jude let Salome enter first and the two followed Yana deeper into the house.

With a flick of her finger, Yana pointed to a small room.

Jude stopped at the opening to see Arava standing alone in what appeared to be a room she shared with her two remaining sisters. Their lavish belongings were strewn about the chamber. Several ornate tunics hung all over. Bronze mirrors, cosmetic vessels, and combs were stacked on a nearby table. Bright veils hung from the ceiling, separating spaces. Jude felt as if he were entering a bridal chamber.

"I'll be working in the other room." Yana continued down the hallway. "See yourselves out when you're done."

Jude shot a desperate look at his sister.

Salome walked into the room and inclined her head toward Arava.

With uneasy steps, Jude followed but kept some space between himself and the women. He attempted to read Arava's countenance but her face was a mixture of frightened animal and Roman stoic statue.

Salome made her way across the room and stood in front of Arava. "You remember my brother, Jude?" She gestured to her forehead and then to Jude.

Arava nodded.

"We've come to see you." She motioned in the space between Jude and herself, up to her eyes, and then back to Arava.

The younger woman nodded again.

"Jude has a question." Salome pointed to her brother and then moved the top part of a single finger up and down.

Arava's attention shifted to Jude.

"Oh." Jude was at a loss. He didn't know how the women communicated with each other. Yana had warned him that simply speaking was not a guaranteed form of being understood. He had not been taught what her gestures meant or how to use them. With desperation, he stepped forward and faced Salome. "I don't know how to talk to her. That's why I brought you."

Salome rested her hand on his cheek and pushed his face toward Arava. "She needs to see your mouth but I can help make sure she understands."

Jude gave into his sister's adjustment and let out a heavy breath. "I want her to come with us." He looked deeper into Arava's eyes. "To see Peter and ask for healing."

Salome did her best to gesture Jude's request.

Arava's eyes grew large, and she shook her head.

Without spoken words, Salome gestured quietly to her.

Again, Arava shook her head. She dug her fingers into her chest.

"What did you say?" Jude asked.

"I asked her why she refuses to come with us."

"And?"

Salome studied Arava's repeated gestures. "I think she's afraid."

The faces of Chislon and Saul filled Jude's vision and caused his throat to burn. "Of her family?"

Salome asked the same question with her signs.

Arava nodded. She also used her finger to poke at unseen spots across her chest.

"And Caiaphas," Salome interpreted.

Jude kept his eyes on Arava. "Tell her she doesn't have to be afraid."

Salome gestured with conviction.

"Tell her if she comes with us and Peter heals her, she won't have to be afraid anymore."

Salome repeated the request.

Arava lifted her hands and gestured swiftly.

Jude watched Arava's hands move in a fluid rhythm as if they were dancing. "What is she saying?"

Salome interpreted, "I can't hear. I can't speak. They don't see me. I'm hidden. Rejected. I'm not counted."

Arava grunted as she pointed to herself.

Jude thought back to the moment several weeks ago in Ethan's synagogue when he'd been rejected by the elders and all the other moments of his life in which he'd been overlooked. He hurt for her. He ached to take away the sting she must feel that he had felt himself. "You," he pointed to Arava then huffed in frustration. He turned to his sister. "How do you gesture 'count'?"

Salome held out one open hand and then used the first finger of her other to press each finger.

Jude studied the movement. He turned to Arava and pointed again at her. "You," he slowly spoke the word. "Count." He imitated Salome's gesture.

Arava shook her head.

Jude repeated the two gestures together. "You. Count."

Arava shook her head slower as tears streamed down her face.

Jude gestured the same two words again and again. He stood there vowing to himself that he would gesture the only two words he knew how to communicate to her until she believed them.

Rivers of tears formed on Arava's cheeks.

"Ask her again," Jude demanded.

Salome gestured 'come' and then 'Peter.'

Arava held Jude's gaze for what seemed to him like hours.

Finally, she dropped her head with a slight nod.

"We need to get to the Temple." Jude stepped toward the door. "Peter will be there for prayer."

Salome held out an open hand to Arava.

The young woman looked around.

Salome coaxed her with a repeated open and close gesture of her hand.

Arava slid her hand into Salome's and followed them out of the room and into the streets of Jerusalem.

CHAPTER 20

Jude pushed through the crowds with only the gleaming Temple in his sights. He didn't dare a glance back as he might give Arava a chance to hesitate and return home.

The sun settled into a lower place in the sky as the hour of prayer came upon the city. Many devout worshippers made daily visits to the Temple during the designated prayer hours resulting in the courtyard being busier during certain times of the day.

As they approached Solomon's porch, Jude saw a gathering forming around his brother's disciples. A glint of metal caught his eye and he turned to see the breastplate of a Temple guard. His back ached with the remembrance of the beating from which he'd only just healed. His heart pounded in his chest as he continued to press forward. Nothing was going to stop him from bringing Arava to Peter.

In the center of the crowd was the older fisherman. His voice carried over the chaos that was religious life happening throughout the Temple.

Jude waited until Peter's lesson was complete before he came forward.

"Jude." Peter's face lit up. "Look at this crowd."

The younger man kept his eyes forward. "I have someone here to see you."

"Who?"

Jude turned around and reached out to Arava.

The woman kept behind Salome's left shoulder, her eyes darting wildly.

He turned back to Peter. "She's in need of healing."

Peter gazed around him. "Come forward, child."

Arava set large eyes on Salome.

She motioned to Peter with a dip of her head.

Jude held out his hand again and made the same motions Salome had earlier in her home to get her to follow them. He opened and closed his fingers together several times.

With extreme hesitation, Arava took a few small steps forward to place herself about two arm's lengths from Peter.

People moved aside to create an open path between them.

With a large step, Peter cleared the space and stooped to look Arava in the eyes. "You've not known much compassion in your young life." He raised his hands to her ears. "In the name of Jesus, hear and speak."

"What is the meaning of this!" a man's voice cried out around them.

Jude spun on his sandals to meet the inflamed gaze of Saul. His stomach flopped.

Saul pushed people aside in an attempt to get closer to his sister. "What is going on here?"

Peter moved to face Saul head-on. "This woman has come forward to receive healing."

"No one needs your deceits and false hopes, old man."

Jude saw Peter's jaw tighten in an attempt to remain calm. He'd known the same frustrations in his dealings with the arrogant tentmaker.

"You'd deny this woman?" Peter challenged.

"You'd blaspheme Adonai with claims of healing in a traitor's name?"

Jude's face burned with heat. He puffed out his cheeks in anger.

Saul came within a hand's breadth of Peter's face. "Why don't you leave Jerusalem and go back to fishing where you belong."

Peter's brow came down in irritation.

Jude could only imagine the thoughts that stayed locked behind the older man's closed lips. He was probably thinking the same ones himself. His gaze flicked to Arava. Confusion and fear were clear on her face. Jude's heart dropped when he realized she was desperately trying to see her brother's mouth because she could not hear the exchange. Peter's prayer had not worked on her.

With frustration and disappointment bringing him to a breaking point, he stepped between Peter and Saul, leveling a challenging glare at Saul. "Why don't you go back to your booth and let Adonai's work be done here."

The sides of Saul's neck grew crimson. "Guards!"

Temple guards descended upon the crowd.

People shouted as they scattered to clear the porch in the wake of the officials.

Saul pointed to Jude and Peter. "Arrest these two for teaching in the name of Jesus."

Before Jude could flee, strong hands were once again around his arm muscles. His gaze fell on Arava as Saul grabbed her wrist and dragged her away. Jude flailed against the hold of the guard as he was pulled in the opposite direction toward the Chamber of Hewn Stone.

There was barely enough day left for their case to be brought before the Council but they were hauled into the semi-circled room anyway.

Jude wasn't sure if he should count himself favored for a quick trial just yet as he and Peter were set before Caiaphas.

The older man combed through his white beard with his fingers as if he were choosing his words carefully before speaking. "Charges?"

A guard stepped forward with Saul.

Jude searched but couldn't see Arava with them.

He'd hoped she was safe but wondered what her brother had done with her. The thought of any harm coming to her on his account inflamed his rage. He set a warning glare on Saul.

The Pharisee-in-training ignored the attempt at intimidation and bowed before the High Priest. "These two were teaching in the name which you forbade them."

Caiaphas shot a glare at Peter.

The fisherman stood straight as an arrow.

Jude wondered if the older man's back burned as much as his did from simply standing in the same spot where they had received their lashes only weeks prior.

The High Priest leaned forward. "Did we not command you to cease teaching in this name?"

Jude followed Peter's lead of keeping his mouth shut. He glanced at Saul and noticed the man nearly salivating over the moment. The sickening grin plastered on his face twisted Jude's innards. He'd like nothing more than an opportunity to remove it.

"We cannot stop doing the work which Adonai has called us," Peter's voice was bolder than his frame.

Caiaphas let his gaze move on from Peter for a moment.

Jude found himself under the scrutinizing glare of the Priest. His resolve shook under the weight of it.

"Is this not the man who has been seeking to become a Rabbi?"

Jude's throat burned as he dipped his head.

"One should be careful what one teaches," Caiaphas warned with a click of his tongue. "Many have stood where you stand now, and time has revealed their false teachings."

Jude nearly allowed a laugh of mockery to burst forth. The irony lay heavy on him like a wool cloak. The members of the council had paved the path for many false teachers among their ranks while warning those who speak truth to cease or face lashes.

His gaze brushed the gathering. They sat like wolves hiding among a flock having clothed themselves in the skin of their prey like Jacob when he deceived his brother for his birthright. How many were waiting for the right moment to rip into the next weak or wayward sheep?

"If one wishes to become a good Rabbi," Caiaphas emphasized his words, "he must teach in accordance with the Law of Moses and the Prophets. Not in the name of their own kin."

Jude felt ready to spit. If they only realized his brother was the Messiah they'd longed for, they would not speak in such a way. Yet, if they understood Jesus is Messiah, they would not have handed him over to Rome in the first place.

"I think a few nights in shackles would do much to teach our young student here a valuable lesson." Caiaphas motioned for a guard to remove Jude. "And take the fisherman with you. Perhaps they could both use a reminder of our order."

Guards escorted Jude and Peter underground.

The steps leading down into the common prison felt all too familiar under Jude's feet. He'd hoped his next visit would be providing food and balms to those held in chains. It seemed for this night, and the next few, he would be the one in chains.

In a small room, the soldiers placed the men's arms and hands in metal restraints that hung from the walls.

When they left with a click of the lock, darkness crept in around Jude. He hung his head. "I don't understand."

Peter's chains clinked as he adjusted. "Why you're here beside me?"

Jude shook his head. His chains clanked with the movement. "Why Arava didn't receive healing? I thought for sure if I brought her to you, you would be able to heal her."

"I don't heal anyone."

"I know it's Adonai," Jude admitted. "But He's done so many healings through you. Even people who simply lay in your shadow." He looked at the fisherman. "Why not Arava? Why wasn't she healed?"

"Do you believe her faith too weak or Adonai too unwilling?"

"I don't know." Jude shrugged as his restraints rubbed against his skin. He laid his head back against the cold wall of his cell.

"'The secret things belong to Adonai.'"

Jude recognized Moses' words though they brought him little comfort.

CHAPTER 21

A few weeks later, Jude stood in the inner courtyard of the Temple staring at the ground. The cell he had shared with Peter lay somewhere under his feet. A cool gust reminded him of the chill of the three long nights he'd spent with his wrists and ankles in chains.

Caiaphas had called for them and released the two with another warning to hold their tongues. They'd since been much more careful about where they spoke Jesus' name by adding more houses to their rotations of places they taught. Solomon's porch was now mostly used to meet with those who were curious and had questions. While the number of needy in Jerusalem grew, the opportunity to teach while administering aid grew along with it.

Jude had been able on several occasions to share his brother's lessons with home groups. The disciples were already spread thin through the city, and he'd spent several nights listening to his mother's recollections of the days she'd spent traveling with Jesus. While visiting widows, injured, and ill, he repeated the lessons and added in his own discoveries from his studies with Rabbi Ethan.

He looked up in time to catch the raising of the antelope's horn. The straight shofar with its gold mouthpiece was blown only one day a year in place of the curled ram's horns with the silver mouthpieces that typically sounded in the Temple. On either side of the priest stood two others with silver horns lifted to their lips. They each blew one short note while the antelope shofar sounded a long note held even after the silver horns were silenced. The unique call signaled the first day of the month of Tishri; the Feast of Trumpets. It was the end of the harvest and the beginning of ten days of preparations for the Day of Atonement.

As the sound resonated through Jude, he took time for self-examination. Each man standing around him was called to do the same. He'd stood in the same courtyard on numerous occasions listening to the instruments of their ancestors. This time felt different.

His previous introspections had held his actions in comparison to the Law of Moses. He reflected on how well he'd kept the Law and the places he'd fallen short. He made vows to do better. Each year falling short of the promises.

This year, while he knew he'd broken the law probably more than any other year of his life, he'd drawn closer to Adonai than ever before. The incredible opportunities to study Ethan's scrolls had shown him more places he missed the mark; at the same time, he'd seen Messiah among the lines. Instead of repenting for those missed marks, he grieved for the lost years he'd spent not understanding his brother's work. Adonai had been gracious to him, and he vowed to make each day of this new year count by boldly sharing about Jesus with anyone willing to listen. Regardless of the results. He'd already endured lashes and chains. What else could Caiaphas do to him?

When the sound of the shofar ended, the people around him shouted.

Jude added his voice to the praise as he watched offerings be brought forward and meticulously sacrificed to Adonai. Each animal and grain had been inspected for perfection and carefully chosen for the fire. Their offering sent up smoke in the hopes that Adonai would be pleased with the gifts.

As a collection of priests came forward with the drink offering to add to the sacrifices, they chanted from the psalm of Asaph, "'Sing aloud to Adonai our strength; shout for joy to the God of Jacob! Raise a song; sound the tambourine, the sweet lyre with the harp. Blow the trumpet at the new moon, at the full moon, on our feast day.'"

The people's praise lifted through the rest of the psalm while the priest performed their ritual duties and musicians obeyed the call of David's chief musician.

Jude listened to the familiar words as each promise of Adonai sunk a little deeper into his soul.

The morning festivities came to a close with the

last portion of the psalm chanted by the priests, "'But he would feed him with the finest of the wheat, and with honey from the rock I would satisfy you.'"

You satisfy, Adonai. Jude whispered from his soul. *Only You satisfy.*

With the first portions of rituals complete, those around Jude moved on with their day. Many of them would return later to join in the evening sacrifices and add their voices to the celebration.

Jude walked toward the steps he'd descended both as a prisoner and as a freeman. It had taken many more talks to convince James to allow him to visit those in chains after he'd been locked away for a second time.

For the first few days after his return to the villa, James had banned him from setting foot in the Temple at all. It was only Jude's persistence that had worn his older brother down enough to allow him to participate in Temple activities once again and permit him to bring provisions to those in need. His second stay in a cell had only solidified his desire to aid those in chains.

Taking the steps with care, he patted the bag that lay across his body. The women had packed it full of food, balms, clean linens, and a skin of fresh water. Though he wasn't supposed to make a visit today. The Feast of Trumpets was a day set aside for leisure and celebration. A grand feast awaited him upon his return to the villa. No doubt the others had returned already and started their merriment. Jude couldn't enjoy a day of rest knowing there were those who celebrated from behind barred doors.

Two guards were posted at the bottom of the steps. He was thankful they were Temple guards who required no enticement for his passage. Only a foolish Hebrew would be caught visiting those in chains, for doing so added the prisoner's shame on the freeman. The same was true of those held in the Roman prison not far away. Yet, Jude had discovered the Roman guards required a bribe to visit their charges. Something Jude was still trying to convince James was worth the price.

He passed the guards without a glance hoping his show of confidence would not raise their suspicion. With haste, he came to the first cell and called, "Shalom."

A shaky "S-S-Shalom" echoed back.

"Are you bound?"

The sound of metal rustling gave Jude his answer before the man could confirm. He hesitated. His previous visits had been focused on those who simply awaited their time before the council. Those who could take freely from his supplies between the bars on the doors. Providing aid to someone who was chained to the wall would prove much more difficult.

He shot a glance at the guards. His stomach flipped. He hoped they would not recognize him as one who had been a resident of their accommodations twice before.

With his resolve firming even among fear, Jude walked to the nearest guard. "Can you open the door?" He held up his pack. "I would like to administer aid to my friend."

The man clad in armor looked Jude up and down before glancing at the other guard.

With a slight nod, the soldier granted consent.

The first guard slipped a large iron key from his waist and unlocked the door. "Be quick about it or I might grow weary and shut this door."

Jude nodded in understanding and slipped through the open door.

In the dim, a man hung from metal shackles. His body frail from malnourishment and abuse provided evidence that he had been there for some time.

Knowing time was his enemy, Jude set down his sack and got to work. "I'm called Jude." He took a clean cloth and wiped at the man's wrists and ankles. They were coated in blood and had open sores. "What are you called?"

"Levi."

"Well, Levi, I'm here to help."

He slowly lifted his head. "W-W-Why?"

CHAPTER 22

Jude took out a small vessel of precious balm and slathered the ointment on the man's open wounds as best he could. "Because my brother told me to do so."

"Ha." Levi sneered. "Who would require such a thing of their sibling?" He winced at the application of the herbal mixture.

Returning the vessel to his bag, Jude retrieved the waterskin and lifted it to the man's cracked lips. "Drink."

Levi parted his lips to receive the water in two large gulps.

"My brother's name is Jesus."

"The one they crucified as King of the Jews?"

"The same." Jude reached into his sack for one of the loaves of bread and tore a large chunk. He fed small pieces as quickly as Levi could eat them. "My brother wore shackles like yours. He was arrested for crimes he didn't commit."

"I said the same."

Jude brushed off the mocking comment. "Jesus was sent by Adonai to show us how to live. He paid the way back to Adonai by His blood and lived a life in the care of those in need. His followers try to live the same life." He lifted the skin again to the man's lips and allowed him a long draw of the fresh water. From recent experience, he knew it would be the only fresh water he'd get while in the custody of Caiaphas.

"Why would you follow in the steps of a man who was killed for his teachings?"

Jude set the seal back in the neck of the waterskin and glanced over the man to see what more he could offer. "Because he lay in a tomb for only three days before rising again."

Levi's eyes widened. "You believe that rumor?"

Jude lifted a shoulder. "Not at first. But then I saw him with my own eyes."

"You've seen a dead man?"

"I can assure you Jesus is not dead."

"Then why did he send you here instead of coming himself?"

In all the conversations he had with people in recent months, Jude had yet to be asked such. "While my brother was here, he traveled around teaching and healing. After he rose from the dead, he spent more time teaching. Then there came a day in which he returned to Adonai. As he did, he commissioned us to do the same work he had done. We teach and heal in his name."

"And what will it get you?"

Jude hesitated as the guard's warning circled his

thoughts. "Nothing."

Levi huffed.

"We don't do any of this for ourselves. We do it for those in need. People like you, Levi."

In the silence, Jude could see the man consider his words. He hoped this time they would not fail as they had when he'd shared the same with Salvus.

"If what you say is true, then may I ask you something else?"

Jude nodded as he packed his bag and moved toward the open door.

"My mother is a widow. She has no one but me to care for her. I don't know how much longer I will be held here, and it's already been a long time since I've been home. Will you visit her?"

"It would be an honor." Jude felt warmth spread through him. Even if Levi didn't fully understand his message, at least he understood the offer of aid. "Tell me where she resides, and I will personally see to her."

"Today?"

"Oh." Jude faltered. "It's the Feast of Trumpets."

A trumpet blast from above confirmed his claim.

"So I've heard." Levi pulled at his restraints. "It would mean a great deal to me if I know she is well."

Jude considered the man's desperation. If his mother had been left alone while he was held in chains, he would have wanted someone to visit her and see to her wellbeing. Thankfully, his mother, though a widow as well, had a whole villa full of people who adored her. He nodded. "Today. Yet I can't guarantee when I can visit you again."

"Thank you." He sighed in relief and rested his weight on the chains.

Jude backed out of the cell. "May Adonai grant you peace."

"And you."

As Jude exited the cell, the guard shut and locked the door behind him. With another visit added to his day, he passed out the rest of the provisions he had brought to those waiting for their cases to be heard as quickly as he could. With the feast day upon them, it would be at least one more night before the council would meet again in the morning to hold trials. These people would endure while others celebrated.

With an empty sack but a full spirit, Jude ascended the steps and set his feet toward the villa. He'd have to return there first in order to refill his bag of supplies before following the directions to the widow's home. Feasting would have to wait a little while longer for him until he fulfilled his promise to the prisoner.

The villa was alive with celebration when Jude entered. Food filled low tables, drink filled stone cups, and music filled the open area. The men had left the Temple right after the morning sacrifices to join the women while Jude had made his visits to the prisoners. Laughter and merriment bounced around the open spaces as disciples, family, and servants alike enjoyed the day of feasting.

Passing the pile of offerings, Jude grabbed a handful of nuts and made his way toward the kitchen.

The room was empty of workers as the day called for rest from work. Though the previous day had contained enough work for two days in preparation. He rifled through vessels and stacks attempting to decide what a widow might need.

"Jude?"

He spun to find Salome behind him.

"What are you doing?" She glanced down at his partially filled bag. "You're not returning to the common prison today, are you?"

Jude swallowed his mashed almonds. "No." He shoved an unleavened loaf into his sack.

"Jude," she rolled her eyes, "you are supposed to be fasting from work."

"I just have one short visit to make."

She set her hands on her hips. "You've already been to see prisoners. Where are you going now?"

He tucked a jar of preserved figs beside the loaf of bread. "One of the prisoners asked me to visit his widowed mother."

"She can't wait until tomorrow?"

He shook his head. "He was adamant that I see her today."

"At least allow me to accompany you."

"No." He waved his palms at her. "It will be a quick visit. If there is anything she needs that I cannot supply from my pack, then we can return another day."

She lifted a curious brow at him.

"If we are both missing from the feast, James might ban me from visiting the prison again. If I go by myself, I can make the excuse that I got held up upon my return. Besides, how can I enjoy the rest of the day knowing that poor woman is all alone?"

Salome dropped her arms in defeat.

He leaned over and kissed her cheek. "Thank you, sister."

She huffed. "You better get back here as soon as you can before James finds you absent."

Jude hummed in agreement as he took stock of what he had already shoved into his bag. "Can you think of anything else a widow might need?"

Salome looked around. "Here." She pushed a wrapped date cake at him. "And add my prayers for her along with it."

He accepted the round gift and tucked it among the other supplies before sneaking back through the celebration and out of the villa.

CHAPTER 23

The streets of Jerusalem were fairly quiet except for the periodic blasts of the shofar.

Jude knew the sound would resonate consistently throughout the day while people enjoyed rest and celebrations in their homes. He made his way through the narrow streets of the Lower City repeating Levi's instructions on how to find the man's home.

When he saw the small courtyard containing a lone woman, he hoped he'd discovered the correct dwelling. "Peace to this house," he called as he approached her.

She rose from a stone bench. "Shalom."

"I am a friend of your son, Levi." Jude hesitated at the low gate. "He sent me to check on you."

"Levi?" Her eyes misted. "Is he well?"

The image of the weak and filthy man hanging from metal chains was one he was glad this poor woman didn't have to witness for herself. "He's well."

She moved toward the gate. "He's been gone so long. When will he return?"

"I'm not sure." Jude rubbed the back of his neck. "He asked me to visit you." He lifted his pack. "I brought you some provisions."

"How kind." She opened the gate. "What are you called?"

"I'm Jude."

She put a hand on her chest. "Orna."

"I bring these gifts in the name of Jesus."

"Jesus?"

Jude stopped mid-step. Her reaction was so mixed, he wasn't sure what to say next.

"That poor man they crucified for teaching we should love each other?"

He let out a slow breath of relief. "He's my brother."

"I'm so sorry. Your family must miss him very much to be doing such acts in his name."

Jude smiled. She was partially correct. He did miss his brother but the acts were done out of wanting to be like his brother and obedient to Adonai. "Have you heard that my brother rose again after three days?"

"I had." She nodded. "It sounds too good to be true."

"It's true." He moved toward the bench. "He is the Messiah our people have longed for."

"I've heard many say he came in the power of Elijah. I wish I had the opportunity to meet him."

He set his bag down and pulled out the cake. "This is from my sister, sent along with her prayers for your family. She wanted you to celebrate the Feast of Trumpets even if you didn't have anyone to feast with you."

Orna accepted the bundle and pulled it close to her chest.

Jude set the other provisions out on top of the stone. "I wasn't sure what need you had so I brought a little bit of everything. If you are lacking anything else, please let me know, and I can bring them back on another day."

"This is so generous." Orna glanced at the pile of gifts. "I don't think I will be able to repay such kindness."

"No payment required." Jude attempted to reassure her. "We have many who give funds so that we can help those in need. My siblings and I visit and provide for several widows in the city. Jesus commanded that we teach the things he shared and continue to care for those in need."

She was quiet for several moments before asking, "Do you only care for widows?"

"No." Jude's brow furrowed. "I often visit those in chains. We've also cared for the sick and injured."

Orna tapped on the cake as she stared down at the supplies filling her bench.

"Something wrong?"

"No." She tapped out another rhythm with her fingers. "You've brought such an offering, I'm not sure if I should ask for more."

"I told you, if there is another need you have,

please tell me. My brothers and I are skilled craftsmen, and we have many others who have strong backs."

"Oh," she shook her head, "it's not for me."

"You know of someone else in need?"

"I'm not entirely sure."

Jude wondered at her hesitation to speak. "If there is someone in need, we can often help."

"It seems so." She lifted her gaze. "The past few days I've seen a woman. At least I believe it's a woman. She scurries around more like a beaten dog." Orna shook her head. "She seems wild and frightened. I don't know if you could help her."

"Where have you seen her?"

"Down there," she pointed to the south, "behind the Inn. The wife of the innkeeper tosses her scraps into their garden for her animals. I've seen the wild woman dig through there but she doesn't let anyone get close to her."

Jude considered the despair of a woman forced to pick through refuse and steal from animals to have a meal.

"She's far too young to be on her own," Orna continued. "I fear for her."

"Do you know anything else about her?"

She looked down at the package in her hand. "One of the other women thought she might have been disowned by her family. Said she looked familiar but wasn't sure." She lifted her gaze. "Do you think you could help her?"

"I can certainly try."

Orna lifted on her toes and glanced around him. "You might get your chance. That's the Innkeeper's wife now dumping out her refuse vessel."

Jude caught a glance of the woman spreading scraps into the garden. He turned back to Orna. "It was a pleasure meeting you. I will be sure we come to see you again until your son can be returned to you."

"May Adonai continue to bless you, Jude."

He bowed and left her small courtyard before heading toward the back of the Inn. Pressing up against a nearby wall, he watched the wife return inside her home. He glanced up one street and down the other. Hardly a person traveled by.

When he was almost ready to give up and return to the villa, a lone figure came toward the garden. The small frame of a woman was hunched and shaking under a thin cloak. The material was pulled up over her head obscuring her face. She walked through the mud and searched the fresh pile of refuse. Her hands were thin and trembling in the cool muck.

Jude's gaze moved up her arm and tried to catch a glimpse of her face under the covering hanging low over her eyes.

She moved just enough for him to see her face for a moment.

"Arava?" He pressed off the wall and made his way

slowly toward her. She would have no way of hearing his calls, and he didn't want to frighten her if she didn't see him.

As he moved ever closer, he chided himself for not taking Salome's offer to accompany him on this visit. He only knew a few of the woman's signs and nothing that would help him at the moment.

He stood behind her as she continually swept her fingers through the discarded waste. The young woman who had known the luxury of a Roman household now appeared sunken and hollowed from begging in the streets. He wondered just how long she'd been living in this lowly state. His heart tore in two as he watched her. What could have happened to bring her here?

With easy steps, he moved enough to catch her field of vision.

She froze.

Jude remained still. He wanted to shout peace at her but knew his voice would only fall on her deaf ears.

Arava slowly raised herself, clinging to the pieces of scraps she collected in the fold of her cloak she'd fashioned as a crude bag. She stood still with her head dipped low for several heartbeats before her slim arm came up toward him.

"She hasn't seen it's me," Jude said, more to himself. "She's asking for coins." His eyes burned at the filth covering her delicate hand.

CHAPTER 24

Instead of filling her hand with silver, he carefully reached out to lift her chin and forced her eyes upon him.

When her gaze came up to meet his, her dark eyes grew as large as platters. She jerked her head away and turned to flee.

Jude put a hand on her arm to catch her. "Stop."

She grunted and pulled against him. Her nails dug into his skin.

A shofar blast sounded around them.

Jude looked up toward the sound and then back down to Arava who hesitated for a moment in her struggle against him. "The blast." He held onto her. As slippery as she was from the mud, he outmatched her strength at least five times. "She can't hear it, but she must *feel* the sound of the shofar."

He reached for her chin again but she resisted his touch. The split in his heart widened. His mind spun with possible ways to communicate with her. How was she going to know he meant no harm when she refused to look him in the face? Without a better idea, Jude slid his hand down her arm, grabbed ahold of her wrist, and lifted her hand to his mouth. "Stop."

She froze.

His heart lifted. At least he'd grabbed her attention. Holding her fingers to his lips, he mouthed, "Arava."

Her body was as stiff as a sculpture.

Jude tried again, "Arava."

As her head turned slowly toward him, large tears fell onto her cheeks.

Jude's insides ached. He gently released his hold on her, hoping she'd stay still long enough for him to try to communicate. Putting both palms up, he slowly asked, "Why?"

Single tears shifted into two streams racing down her face. She lifted one finger and traced lines across her forehead.

He shook his head. "I don't understand." Frustration rose in him like a priest lifting a shofar toward the sky. His concern for the answer to his question shifted into the need to get her off the streets as quickly as possible. Glancing toward the upper city, he bent down to look her in the eyes. He formed each word as slowly as he could, "I...take...you...home."

Her eyes widened further, and she turned to run again.

Jude caught her arm. "Wait."

She thrashed and grunted.

"Arava, please." He pulled her into himself.

She beat her fists against his chest.

"Stop." He lifted her off the ground.

She tensed in his grasp.

He shook his head. The stoic Roman statue look she held on her face was one he was growing to hate. He slowly lowered her back to her feet. Releasing only one hand, he held his palm up to her and opened and closed his fingers. "Come."

She shook her head.

"Salome." He couldn't think of anyone she trusted more, except her own sister, but he couldn't remember the way to the home where Talia now resided. "Salome." He tried again to make her understand. "I...take...you...to...Salome."

Arava's brows hunched down over her eyes.

He felt as if he were speaking to a small child for as much progress as he was making and the mounting frustration. "My sister." He put his hand on his chest. "I'll take you to my sister."

Something close to realization dawned on her face and she eased, but only slightly.

"Good." He sighed. "We're getting somewhere." He opened and closed his fingers again. "Come. Salome."

She nodded.

Jude considered keeping one hand firmly on her wrist so she couldn't try to run again but he thought it best to show her a little trust. He gradually let each finger off her arm and held up both of his empty hands.

She looked at her arm and back at him.

He winced thinking he had harmed her in their heated exchange. Shame crept up his neck. He moved to stand beside her and faced the direction of the villa. With his open hand, he gestured 'come' again.

Arava held her cloak against herself.

Before he took the first step, Jude remembered the scraps she had collected. "Leave it." He pointed to the bundle in her cloak.

She looked down and back up at him.

"Leave it." He reached for the end of the cloak.

She pulled it tighter to her chest.

He grabbed the end of the material and yanked it open, causing the refuse to fall out around their feet.

She grunted at his force and smacked his hand.

"I know you don't understand." He dropped the now empty material. "But there is a feast waiting for us. You don't need these scraps."

Arava gazed down at the pieces of rejected food.

"You don't need it, Arava," he grumbled. "There is a feast waiting for you."

She furrowed her dirty brow at him.

He held up his hand and opened and closed his fingers. "Come."

She glared at him but cautiously followed his steps.

The journey to the villa was made in silence. Jude rebuked himself all the way there for his harshness with the young woman. He knew she must be frightened but he was at a loss in his attempts to communicate with her. After he made sure she was safe and fed, he'd have to ask Salome how to apologize to Arava.

The closer they got to the villa, the more she seemed to ease. Though she occasionally glanced over her shoulder.

"What has brought her to this state?" Jude wondered out loud knowing she couldn't hear his mutterings. "Hopefully Salome can get her to say."

The celebration was still at its height when Jude showed Arava into the villa. Music rang off the stone walls and laughter and chanting added to the joyous melody.

Arava pressed close to him as they moved deeper into the large estate.

Jude felt a touch of delight at her choice to move closer to him. He'd hoped she was learning to trust him as her ally and not as the rough man he'd been moments before.

She kept to his back as they searched the crowd for Salome.

Jude waded through the people not revealing his foundling or stopping enough for anyone to ask after her. Realizing Salome was not in the courtyard with the others, he moved toward the only other place he thought she'd be on this feast day.

In the kitchen, he found his youngest sister

refilling a tray with piles of fresh fruit.

Salome set harsh eyes on Jude when he entered, but gasped when she saw the condition of Arava. "What happened to her?" She rushed across the room.

"I don't know." Jude stepped aside so Salome could examine her. "I found her like this."

"You poor thing." Salome lifted the younger girl's arms. "You're filthy."

"I was hoping you could talk to her and get her to tell you what happened."

Salome enveloped Arava in her arms. "No matter what it is, she is safe now."

Jude felt a sense of peace wrap around him as he watched his sister's immediate care for the lost lamb. His mood shifted. "Salome?"

She looked over at him.

"Tell her I'm sorry."

She lifted a curious brow as she glanced between the two of them.

"I had to be pretty harsh to get her here." He rubbed the back of his neck. "She was rather frightened when I discovered her."

"That's understandable considering her state." She looked her up and down. "I wonder how long she's been like this."

"I trust you to find out what happened so we can set things right."

Salome nodded. "First, I'll get her cleaned up and

get some food into her. She looks as frail as a neglected mule."

"I'll leave her with you. Come find me when you're done." He moved toward the door. "I get the pleasure of breaking the news to James about the possibility of another wayward house guest."

CHAPTER 25

Jude's search for James was fruitful. The older brother was fully enjoying the day of rest and merriment. Jude couldn't blame him. A lot weighed on the shoulders of his brother, and he deserved this break as much as anyone. "Could I have a word?"

"Jude!" James slapped his brother's back. "I wondered if you'd lost your way." He laughed so hard he doubled over.

The burn of the slap on his still-tender skin made Jude jump. A glance into James' half-empty cup caused him to wonder if the brother was enjoying his day of rest a little too much.

James pointed to Elissa. "My dear wife has the most wonderful news."

Jude flicked his gaze to his sister-in-law.

She held her hands behind her back and fixed a wide smile on her face.

James put his arm around Jude's shoulders and pulled him in close. "She's going to make me a father."

"That's wonderful news." He leaned into his brother's embrace. "May you be blessed with a quiver full."

"Ima is so excited." James waved toward the upper level. "As soon as she heard, she went straight upstairs to start gathering supplies to make garments for the little one."

Jude counted the time since their wedding feast. "But it will still be months before a baby arrives."

"You know Ima." James shook his head. "I only wish Abba were here." He grew mournful. "I really could use his example. I don't know anything about being a father. Jude, how am I going to be a father?"

"Sure you do." Jude patted his brother's arm. "You've had lots of practice ordering all of us around."

James let out a full belly laugh. "That is very true."

"I'm sure you'll make a great Abba."

"You mean that?"

"Of course."

James squeezed Jude's shoulder. "That means a lot."

"May I have that word with you now?"

Lifting the cup to his lips, James nodded for him to speak.

"It seems we might have an addition before your addition arrives."

James took a long draw from his cup before lowering it. "Did Joseph pick up another injured soldier?" He chuckled at his own jest.

Jude glanced toward the kitchen. "Nothing like that."

"Then what?"

"I visited a man in prison this morning who asked me to visit his widowed mother."

"So, a widow?"

Jude shook his head. "The widow told me about a woman who was begging and searching for food near her home."

"Well, that happens a lot in this city." He raised his cup and emptied it.

"It's Arava."

James nearly spit out the mixed wine. Instead, he choked it down. "You're telling me you brought Saul's sister here?" he asked through coughing gasps.

"What was I supposed to do, just leave her out in the streets?"

"Of course not." James pounded his chest to clear his throat. "But she is the daughter of a wealthy family. And one, might I add, whose son is seeking Way Followers to feed to Caiaphas, and you bring his sister to a nest of us. Why didn't you take her back home?"

"I tried, but she refused." Jude lowered his voice. "I think something happened. She was so frightened when I mentioned taking her home."

James took a few steadying breaths and straightened his tunic. "Where is she now?"

"With Salome." Jude motioned over his shoulder with his chin. "I asked her to get Arava clean and some food in her."

"That bad?"

"She was filthy and lean. I'm hoping Salome can find out what happened."

"Do you think she'll tell her?"

"Hard to say." Jude tried to push the possibility of Arava keeping silent about the circumstances that led her away from home from his thoughts. "Salome has a way with her I've only ever seen with Talia."

"Talia!" James shouted. "We could take her to her older sister."

"I didn't remember where she lives." Jude tucked his head. "I was...distracted the night of her wedding feast."

James gave him a knowing look. "I think I remember but let's give Salome a chance to discover why Arava was away to begin with, and then we will attempt to make arrangements. For now," he lifted his cup to his lips, but discovered it void, "let's enjoy the feast."

Later in the evening, Jude watched Salome guide Arava around the tables of food. As the younger woman pointed, Salome laid items on a platter.

Arava's skin was washed, and she wore one of Salome's tunics. The material swept the floor revealing Arava was much shorter than his sister. Judging from the material bunched around the fabric belt it seemed as though they had already attempted to overcome the height difference as best they could.

Jude gradually made his way toward them. He'd already done enough to scare the young woman. He didn't want to add more charges to his negative account with her.

Salome caught his approach first and nodded with a welcoming bow of her head. "She's feeling much better."

Leaving lots of space between himself and the two women, he smiled. "Have you discovered what happened to her?"

Salome's dark eyes dimmed. "I have."

"Is she well?"

"She is now." She reached over and put a handful of figs on the dish.

"What did she say?"

Salome hesitated. She looked at Arava and handed her the plate of food. "Her father sent her away."

"Chislon?" Jude's blood boiled under his skin. "Her own father sent her away?"

"It seems so." She pointed to a place where Arava could sit and eat.

The girl obeyed as she made her way to the seat.

Jude closed the gap between himself and his sister as he followed. "What happened?"

Salome looked up into his eyes, all light had drained out of hers. "Do you remember the day we took her to the Temple?"

"We were trying to take her to Peter for healing.

Even you thought it was a worthy idea."

Salome closed her eyes. "Saul took her home that day and told their father about her going to Peter." She slowly opened them as tears flooded down her face. "They sent her away because they thought she was a Way Follower. She'd already been enough of a stumbling block to Saul's rise in status because of her maladies. I guess they weren't going to let her association with us be the stone that prevented her brother from his seat among the Pharisees."

Jude's neck and chest grew hot. "That...that—" He stormed away mumbling curses under his breath.

"Jude!" Salome raced to keep up with him. "Don't!"

Joseph moved to block his path. "What's going on?"

"Out of my way!" Jude shoved past his brother. He threw all of his force at the beam across the door and lifted it.

"Jude!" James' voice barked over the sounds of celebration. "Halt!"

"Don't try to stop me!" Jude reached for the handle. "I will give that snake a piece of my mind and maybe more."

James and Joseph were behind him, tearing at his shoulders.

The burn of rubbing against his healed wounds caused him to yelp.

"Peace, brother," James ordered.

Jude thrashed against them. "I will not have peace until I deal with that utter snake of a man."

"Peace, I say!"

The door flung open under Jude's pull and a fresh gust pushed cold air against his face. Its icy fingers were enough to stop him, momentarily.

James and Joseph seized the opportunity to pull him back inside.

Men filled the entryway at the commotion.

"Get the door!" James shouted.

Thomas and Andrew set the beam back into place while Peter and John helped the two brothers draw Jude into the villa like a net full of fish.

"Let me go!" Jude demanded.

"Not until you calm." James tightened his grip on Jude's arm.

"It's all my fault." Jude broke out into sobs and crumbled into his older brother's hold. "It's all my fault."

CHAPTER 26

After a fitful night of disappointing sleep, Jude woke to his head pounding and his back burning.

"Here." James stood over him with a cup of water. "Drink."

Jude accepted the small vessel and emptied it in one large gulp. He held the cool stone to his head.

James sat beside him. "Mind telling me what all that was about last night?"

"I figured Salome would have filled you in."

"She did." He hesitated. "I want to hear your side of it."

Jude rolled the stoneware across his forehead attempting to knead the ache away. "It's all my fault."

"What is?"

He set the cup down. "All of it. I convinced Arava to meet with Peter. I thought he could heal her."

"Peter doesn't heal anyone."

Jude huffed. "You know what I meant."

"Continue."

"I thought that if she could meet Peter that Adonai would heal her. Then she wouldn't have to be hidden away."

"Sounds like a worthy attempt."

"I thought so too."

"So, what happened?"

"Nothing."

"Nothing?"

Jude lifted a shoulder. "She met Peter but she wasn't healed."

"And that's all?"

Jude hung his head. "Saul was there. He dragged her away and told Chislon about Arava going to Peter. They think she's a Way Follower so they sent her away." He looked up into his brother's face. "She was living in the streets because I tried to bring her to Peter for healing."

James hummed to himself for several moments. "Perhaps we should speak with Chislon directly instead of trying to take Arava to Talia."

The thought of looking upon Saul's smug face made Jude's stomach turn and his skin feel warm. "I'd love nothing more than to have a word with Saul."

"Chislon." James held up a finger. "We will speak with the girl's father, and you will keep your distance from Saul." He firmed his command with a look of authority. "You've gotten yourself into enough trouble with the council lately."

"I will try."

James dropped his hand. "Maybe we should seek Hiram's help in this matter. They are both tentmaking families."

"Hiram doesn't get along with Saul."

"That's right." James rubbed his temple. "He will only add kindling to this fire." He sighed. "I guess we are on our own with this one."

Jude jumped to his feet. "The market should be open today."

"Don't you want to break your fast first?" James rose with a grunt.

"Not if it means righting this wrong."

"Well, there is no guarantee of that." James put a cautious hand on his brother's shoulder. "Let's at least spend some time seeking Adonai before we go."

Jude bent to his brother's wishes. If Adonai was choosing not to heal Arava, the least He could do was heal the rift in her family.

After a short time of prayer, Jude and James set out for the market.

The streets were alive with activity in the wake of a day of rest. People moved through the pathways like boats at a port city. The market was crowded with buyers seeking the best gains the day held for them and sellers eager to be the ones making a profit.

They came upon Chislon hard at work at his craft. The booth was covered in varying cloths, leathers, and other materials. Some fabrics were solid colors while others were striped. Jude appreciated the display of fine craftsmanship just as he would if he were examining a well-made dwelling. Chislon certainly had talent. Jude hoped he would be as open to resolving this issue of Arava as he was with sharing his work.

"Shalom," James called out on their approach.

Jude thought of a few other choice greetings he'd like to use but held his tongue instead. He was only too glad that Saul was nowhere in sight.

"Shalom." Chislon set his work down and walked toward them. "A fine day for a new tent, is it not?"

James glanced around the booth. "A fine day but we are seeking to speak with you."

Chislon's countenance shifted to one of annoyance.

Jude weighed the change in the man's mood attempting to decipher if Chislon already knew the topic of discussion or if he was disappointed with wasting time on someone who would not be a buyer.

"I'm a very busy man." The tentmaker waved around. "If you're not going to buy anything, then we have nothing to discuss."

"Actually," James moved into the booth, "we do."

Chislon measured the young man with a steely gaze.

"We've come to discuss one of your daughters."

Jude noticed the man flinch.

Chislon searched James. "You think you're worthy to betroth one of my daughters, craftsman?"

James straightened. "I don't come here seeking a

betrothal. I'm happily wed."

"Your brother then." He pointed a long needle toward Jude. "You think him wealthy enough to afford the luxuries to which my daughters are accustomed?"

Jude puffed out his chest but kept his feet firmly planted and his lips sealed like a tomb. His brother had warned him before they left the villa to allow him to handle speaking with Chislon, but the man's arrogance was wearing on Jude's patience which was already as thin as a worn garment.

"We don't come seeking any marriage arrangements." James held up a hand. "We've come to return a daughter to you."

"All of my daughters are where they should be."

Jude bit the inside of his cheek.

"Arava." James let the woman's name drop like a heavy hammer on an anvil.

Jude noticed Chislon flinch again.

He moved away, waving his hand in the air. "I don't have a daughter by that name."

James looked at Jude.

Jude tightened his jaw and ground his teeth desperate to obey James' command to hold his tongue.

James turned back to Chislon. "Your youngest child who is deaf—"

"I have no deaf daughter." Chislon spit to the side. "Get out of my booth." He pushed James. "Go on. Get out of here."

James stumbled into Jude.

Jude caught his brother from falling.

"I don't ever want to see your faces in my booth again." Chislon stomped away.

"What now?" Jude asked his brother.

James straightened his tunic. "Now we go see Talia. And pray she doesn't have her father's temper."

Jude allowed James to lead the way to Raphu's family home. He'd been successful in remaining silent while James spoke with Chislon but his tolerance for the family was fraying like the ends of a worn blanket. He too prayed Talia would hold more compassion than her father.

All he wanted was for Arava to be healed from that which kept her from experiencing a full life. *How could a father simply throw away one of his children for another?* He couldn't grasp the thought much less the actual action. Surely Arava's sister would have pity on her and take her in.

The two turned a corner and came upon a group of women working in a courtyard.

Jude recognized Talia mending a garment. He'd not laid eyes on her since her wedding feast. She'd been radiant in her bridal garments, and he'd wasted the joy of a feast for the sorrow he held. Seeing her sitting among the other women of Raphu's family, he was amazed at how much she seemed to fit like a well-cut stone.

"Peace to this house," James called as he approached the gate.

Talia rose from her place and halted their advance with an upheld hand. "That's far enough."

James flicked a confused glance at Jude. "We only wish to speak."

"I know why you're here." Talia crossed her arms over her chest. "Yana came to see me the other day along with our Ima."

"So, you know what they've done." Jude couldn't help speaking. He'd watched James' attempts at mediation on behalf of Arava fail once today. He wasn't laying his hopes on his brother's words again. He demanded action.

Talia shifted her gaze to him. "Yes."

"What are you going to do about it?"

"Nothing."

Jude saw sorrow cloud her eyes. "You choose to allow your youngest sister to beg in the streets while you sit here mending garments?" He flicked his hand toward the gathering of women.

"You think I have a choice in all this?" Her eyes squinted into narrow lines.

"You do."

"My father has made his will clear." She shook her head. "My husband has also made his will clear."

Jude closed the space between them bringing his face within a hand's width of hers. "You'll let your sister live like a beggar? The sister you claim to love?"

Talia matched his intense glare with one of her own. "I love my sister more than you will ever understand." She flicked a glance at James before returning her strong sight on Jude. "Arava is where Adonai wants her."

For the first time Jude could recall, he felt a guttural growl come up from his bowels. He was beyond the point of frustration. He wanted to pack sense into this family's head like the empty satchels they were. How could he make Talia see that she was Arava's last chance? "How dare you claim Adonai's will to excuse a father's choice to abandon his child all for the sake of status."

Talia recoiled as she dropped her gaze. "Arava is where she's supposed to be."

Jude turned on his heels in maddening defeat. Words were no match for the hardened hearts of Arava's family. He needed to leave before he said or did something he would later regret.

CHAPTER 27

A week later, Jude walked the streets of Jerusalem toward Ethan's synagogue in the rays of early light. His Rabbi had given him the honor of speaking on this, the Day of Atonement. He'd broken his fast early and rushed to be the first in the meager dwelling to spend a few peaceful moments with Adonai before the others arrived.

Smoke rose from the east as the cool morning air carried the scent of sweet incense. The priests were performing their yearly rituals in the inner court to cleanse the sins of the people of Israel. Elaborate ceremonies held in the Temple were meant to display the temporary atonement those who came from Abraham would receive.

Jude paused to stare at the dark column that rose against the bright sky. He thought of the two goats and the bull who'd been chosen so their blood could be sprinkled on the stone where the mercy seat should have sat. The golden box carried through multiple wars and rested in times of peace had long been carried off by an enemy. Its contents and the seat where Adonai met with His people had been replaced by a boulder.

Yet the priests still took the blood offering behind the veil every year to cover the people's sins.

Upon entering the synagogue, he reviewed his thoughts on the scroll from which he'd chosen to read. The important day for his people could bring him to no other place than Moses' instructions to Aaron and the other priests on how this day's sacrifices were expected to be performed.

After the death of the two sons of Aaron. Jude recalled the line that had caused him to pause several times in his studies the previous days. The instructions had been given after Nadab and Abihu had defiled the holy place by offering strange fire of their own accord. Aaron, a father, had lost his two sons before receiving the carefully detailed instructions for how to cover Abraham's children's sins. He couldn't cover the sins of his own children but he would be tasked with covering his people's sins until his death.

Jude paced the bema as thoughts of his teaching mingled with those of Arava. She'd been welcomed into the villa with open arms after Jude and James' attempts to return her to her father and her sister had failed. Salome had taken the younger woman under her wing like a mother hen with chicks. His sister's immeasurable depth of patience had been the very thing to bring Arava from her darkness. Jude had even seen her smile once or twice. The memory brought one corner of his lips upward.

He shook Arava from his mind. She was safe, at least for now. Today was Jude's chance at redemption. The seats around him would not be filled with the most intellectual minds the city had to offer. Instead, the levels would be filled with the willing. Those who would be welcomed in this place even if they were not welcomed anywhere else.

Soaking in Adonai's peace in the quiet moments, Jude prayed for those who would come. He prayed for their hearts and minds to be open. He prayed they would leave encouraged and challenged. Most of all, he prayed his tongue would not be an obstacle to Adonai's words.

The synagogue filled with people before Jude was ready for them. If he were honest with himself, he never felt ready to teach.

His brothers and the disciples took their place among the collection of men while his mother and sisters scooted in next to the other women.

Jude caught Arava press close against Salome. Her eyes darted wildly around the room. She almost always looked frightened, like she was going to flee at any moment. The clear look of anxiety on her face pulled at Jude's heart. He couldn't blame the poor creature. How terrifying it must be to have limited access to the world. An obstacle he had tried desperately to eradicate for her but found that it was impossible to move.

He allowed his gaze to drift to the others gathered

in the one-room dwelling. People from all over the city met here where they knew they would be welcomed. Some who were not welcome in the Temple or even their own homes could gather under this roof and hear Adonai's words. Others came out of duty and still others merely out of curiosity. Still, no matter what brought them there, Ethan's synagogue was a place any and all were welcomed. His gaze fell back on Arava. A place, even if one couldn't hear or speak, they could be present for the reading of Adonai's words. A right that had been withheld from Arava by her family.

The weight of the moment fell heavy on Jude's shoulders. It was an honor; a privilege. A responsibility he carried with awe and reverence.

Ethan came toward him. "Are you ready?"

Jude smiled. "No, but that doesn't matter."

"What does matter, my student?"

He looked back at Arava. "If they are ready to hear."

The older man turned toward the gathering and opened their time with a prayer and a song of praise from David.

When the moment came, Jude cautiously walked toward the ark of scrolls. The looming cabinet still held him entranced no matter how many times he'd pulled open the doors in the fleeting months. He could spend a lifetime studying the words contained within the simple structure and go to rest with his fathers having spent his days in joy.

He retrieved the exact scroll he needed and laid it on the stone table. With caressing fingertips, he unrolled the parchment and found his place in the third book of Moses. He took a breath and read his selected text with as much rhythmic pace as he could assemble. He'd practiced the words in his sleep and kept them at the forefront of his mind for days.

"The Lord spoke to Moses after the death of the two sons of Aaron, when they drew near before the Lord and died," the heart-wrenching words flowed from Jude's mouth. He'd been unsettled by them and wondered how Aaron's heart must have broken at burying his children.

He raised a quick glance at Arava and wondered once more how Chislon could simply toss one of his children aside.

Jude continued as the detailed instructions of the sacrifices to be performed on the Day of Atonement poured forth. He allowed his gaze to come up every now and then to be encouraged by those nodding along as he read the entire passage.

When he finished, he returned the rolled scroll to its proper place and took his seat on the bema. For several moments, he recounted each detail and why the elaborate ceremonies were necessary. He reminded them of the sin of Adam and the sins of their people through the generations.

Then the moment came to draw their attention to the topic upon which he most wanted to focus. "The priests cleansed themselves and put on their holy garments before slaughtering goats and bulls for their blood. They did this at the instruction of Moses.

"Of the two goats selected, one died and one was sent away into the wilderness as still happens to this day. My brother, Jesus, was led out of Jerusalem to die outside the camp just as the sin-bearing goat died in the wilderness outside the camp of Moses."

Jude made sure he faced Arava and spoke slightly slower than his normal pace. He fought his fearful tendency to rush his speech by reminding himself that, though she might not be able to understand everything he was saying, he hoped something made its way past her closed ears and into her soul.

"Jesus removed his holy garments to become the sin offering not only for the children of Israel but for all those who are not numbered among the tribes. His blood was the final sin offering needed to cover our debt. This needed to be done only once and not yearly as we've done since the days of Aaron." He caught the approving nod of Ethan and let it lift his spirit as he continued to teach about Jesus.

CHAPTER 28

Jude tied two strong poles together with a perfect knot. Their family's booth for the Feast of Tabernacles was quickly taking shape with the three brothers working together. James had sent the women to gather branches for the roof while they set up the walls.

With another knot, Jude secured the poles to the ones Joseph had been working on.

"A couple more of these," Joseph pointed to the pair in Jude's hands, "and I think we'll be done with the walls."

"The girls will be back any moment with the fronds." Jude selected another pair of poles. "Then they'll want us to step aside while they decorate the booth."

"Every year." Joseph chuckled. "We do all the heavy lifting, and they simply get to hang colorful veils."

"That's because you wouldn't know which end was up," Lydia commented as she set a large basket of branches at her brother's feet.

Joseph huffed at her.

Jude rolled his eyes at his siblings. They'd had the

same argument every year they'd constructed a booth outside Jerusalem for the holy day. He found it best to let them fight over the construction and decoration.

This feast was Jude's favorite time of year. It was the last High Holy Day for a few months but the entire week was dedicated to his favorite things. After the booth was constructed and decorated with fruit and foliage, the family spent the week sitting, eating, and sleeping in the booth. Best yet, they were required to do nothing but study the teachings of Moses and bring sacrifices to the Temple.

Jude looked down at the makeshift row of booths. Several nearby were constructed by the disciples. He watched the fishermen craft simple structures to house themselves for the coming week. Their plain dwellings visibly lacking without the touch of a woman.

"I think I'll take a walk." He spoke to James. "The women can take over from here." He gave Salome a wink.

"Don't stray too far," his brother warned. "You're to cite the first lessons this evening."

"Wouldn't miss it."

Jude's soul was still lifted from speaking in the synagogue a few days prior. Though he'd still not read perfectly, his ancestral tongue had become easier, and his thoughts had been ordered better than ever. He halted at a booth constructed near Peter's. "Shalom."

"Shalom," Theodotos returned the greeting.

Jude examined the priest's construction. "Fine booth you've made."

"Thank you." He pressed on one of the supporting poles. "It'll do."

Jude bowed to the man's wife who was stringing up a vine. He'd not spent much time with the woman but found her to be as gracious a host as her husband.

Theodotos leaned on the pole. "I wanted to tell you something."

Jude considered what the priest would need to share with him but came up empty. "Oh?"

"Yes." He put his finger and his thumb on either side of his bearded chin. "I've had several talks with Peter lately and have, how did the fisherman put it... 'become obedient to faith in Jesus'."

"Have you?" Jude couldn't believe the declaration. Though they'd seen thousands put their faith in Jesus, the religious leaders had been the hardest to convince. "I'm sure Adonai will use you greatly to testify to others."

The priest nodded. "I also wanted to let your family know that you are welcome to reside in my villa for as long as you'd like."

"That's very gracious."

He suddenly became serious. "Or at least as long as it's safe to do so."

Jude felt a chill in his warning. He'd fallen into such a routine lately that he'd almost forgotten about the threat that hung over them. Even with the ache in his back an inconsistent reminder. They'd not caught Rome's attention as Jesus had done but they were not far from the ever-scrutinizing gaze of the council. He nodded in simple agreement and excused himself.

The colorful booths crowded the sands outside Jerusalem like a flock of sheep in a pasture.

"Jude!"

He turned toward the loud call. "Dod?" Through the shifting sands, he hurried over to his uncle. "It's good to see you."

The larger man embraced him fully. "Shalom, my nephew. Peace to you."

Jude looked into their booth. "Doda." He kissed his aunt on both of her cheeks.

"There is my handsome nephew." Mary pinched his chin and turned his face from side to side. "All these good looks and not a wife to show for it."

Jude's cheeks flushed.

"Enough, woman." Cleophas waved her off. "You're embarrassing the boy."

"Ahh." She waved back at her husband. "He's got all those brains and hasn't been smart enough to find himself a wife yet. There are plenty of good women in Jerusalem, Jude. You should pick one already."

"James keeps me busy."

"And so does your Rabbi, I hear."

Jude rubbed at the back of his neck. "It seems lately

all I've seen are scrolls and widows."

"Well," she patted his cheek, "don't neglect life while you study and serve."

"I'll try to remember that." He rubbed at his cheek. "You should come by our booth this evening. James is letting me do the first reading tonight, and Ima is cooking."

Cleophas spread his arms wide. "Count us in."

Jude left his uncle and aunt's booth to continue his trek through the encampment. He felt as if he were lifted back to the camp of Israel under Moses' command. The gathering of familiar faces comforted his soul.

As his thoughts swirled with the past and present, he laid eyes on an old friend. "Lazarus!"

The man straightened from bending to drive a stake in the sand. He lifted his hammer. "Shalom!"

Jude moved closer to stand under the shade of their booth. "I'm glad you've made the trip from Bethany."

"We wouldn't miss Sukkot." Lazarus tossed his hammer into a pile of tools. "It's Mary's favorite feast."

"Are your sisters here?"

He pointed inside the booth. "I think they are discussing which veils to put up."

"Ah." Jude chuckled. "I just came from the same discussion."

"Jude!" The two women appeared from under the flaps of the booth.

"Shalom." Jude tipped his head to them. "I hope you enjoy the feast."

"Jude," Martha stepped forward, "will you please tell Mary that this blue linen is a much better choice than her red one?"

"Martha, don't bother Jude with such things." Mary shook her head. "Don't answer her, Jude."

He flicked his attention to Lazarus.

The younger brother put up his hands.

"I think they are both lovely." Jude attempted to remain neutral.

The effort was not well received by Martha who put a hand on her ample hip. "You can speak truth. My sister's selection recalls Rahab's cord."

"Martha!" Mary snapped her cloth at her sister. "Don't say such things."

Martha jutted her chin out at her sister. "Well, it does."

The two ducked back into the booth while continuing to argue over cloths.

Lazarus shook his head after them.

Jude lifted a shoulder. "Sisters."

"I wouldn't trade them for the world."

After having made a journey through the temporary city of booths, Jude returned to his own to find his family settled in and a stew boiling over a fire. The familiar scent of his mother's cooking drew him in like a warm embrace.

The evening was filled with recitations and songs as the family enjoyed a peaceful evening under the stars.

Jude laid his head upon his sleeping mat surrounded by his family and one sojourner. He fell asleep praising Adonai for each of his many blessings.

CHAPTER 29

The following morning brought a day of rest and much-needed time among family and friends for Jude. He and his brothers had been invited to gather in Peter's tent while the women went to fetch water for the day.

Jude settled in the booth listening to Peter and James speak. Even during a holy day, the two couldn't seem to set aside their tasks. He didn't fault them. If he'd been given the opportunity, he'd be at the ark of scrolls studying.

Peter paced the small area. "There has been something the men have discussed at great length."

"Something troubles you?" James asked.

"Not so much troubles us but something that has been weighing on us."

"Speak on."

Peter halted. "We've been wanting to call our families to join us here in Jerusalem."

"For the next feast?"

"For as long as Adonai keeps us in Jerusalem."

James rose. "You mean to have your families join you permanently?"

"Passover will be here in a few short months." Peter spread his hands. "If we send a messenger soon, they would have plenty of time to make the necessary arrangements."

"Have you counted the risks?" James cleared the space between them. "You've been arrested twice and received lashes. Would you want your wife to see you endure such?" He turned toward the other men. "Would any of you want your families to see you like that? Or worse, share your fate?"

Peter put a hand on James' shoulder. "I know your words come from concern but your family dwells with you." He looked to Joseph and Jude. "We simply want ours to do the same."

"What about Theodotos? His villa is already filled with many."

"We've spoken." Peter let his hand fall to his side. "Our host has graciously extended an open home to our families. Though we've also discussed the possibility of some of us moving into other arrangements."

James furrowed his brow. "Other arrangements?"

"Still in Jerusalem." He lifted a hand. "There are others who are willing to open their homes to us so that we don't overcrowd the villa."

Joseph stood. "I think it's a wonderful idea."

James shot a glance at his brother.

"Why would we keep families apart?" Joseph

stepped beside Peter. "I hated that Jesus tore ours apart for so long."

James looked at Jude. "Do you have anything to add?"

Jude remained seated. "If I had a wife and family, I wouldn't want to be separated from them for so long." He looked to Peter and the others. "These men have already been away from their families for years. I think reuniting them would be a blessing. And besides," he lifted a shoulder, "more hands would help spread the workload."

James glanced back at Peter. "I wouldn't want to be the one keeping families apart. I simply want you to consider the danger they may be under coming to stay in Jerusalem."

"We understand the risk."

Jude excused himself while the others made plans to extend the invitation to their family members. He'd said his peace and wanted to retreat to the solitude of their booth to rest. This week was about refreshing one's soul from work, not planning more work for when the week was over.

As he came upon his family's booth, he noticed Arava knelt in the sand. Her back was turned to him so he couldn't see what she was doing. With careful steps, he leaned over her, knowing she wouldn't hear him.

In the sands of the earth, she was scribing letters.

He took a step too close and tumbled forward

falling into the dirt next to her.

Arava jumped to her feet.

"Sorry." Jude held up his hands as he made his way to his feet. "I didn't mean to…" He let his apology drop as he brushed off his tunic. "Here I am talking to you like you can hear any of it." He shook his head more at himself than anything.

She leaned away, looking as if she would flee at one more word.

He held out an open palm. "I didn't mean to frighten you." He looked down at the letters. "What are you doing?"

She kept a cautious glare on him.

He pointed to the letters in the sand.

Her gaze slowly lowered and she fell on the dirt, wiping them away as quickly as she could.

"No." Jude reached out for her. "I didn't mean—"

She continued rubbing at the dirt until all traces of her writings were gone.

He stood staring at the swiped sand. "You can write." He allowed a smile to sweep across his face.

Arava stood slowly but kept her head down.

He pointed to the swipes in the sand. "I saw them."

She followed his motion with her eyes but adamantly shook her head.

"You shouldn't have to be ashamed."

When he looked up, her gaze on him was wild and full of fear.

Salome came upon them. "There you are. I've been looking for you." She glanced between Arava and Jude. "Is she well?"

Jude let his gaze drift to his sister. "Did you know she can write?"

Salome faced Arava and made a motion with her finger in the palm of her other hand.

Arava dipped her head.

"I saw." Jude pointed down. "She was drawing letters in the sand."

Salome waited for Arava to lift her eyes before she made more motions to her.

With an unsure glance at Jude, Arava replied with her own gestures.

Jude watched the fluid movements. "What's she saying?"

"She was refused lessons as a child." Salome nodded along with Arava's signs and let out a chuckle.

Jude flicked his gaze to Salome. "What?"

"She would sneak into Saul's things and copy his scrolls in the dirt."

Jude looked upon Arava who was still gesturing to Salome. "They refused her the right to learn simply because she couldn't hear?"

Salome lifted a shoulder. "Perhaps they didn't see the point. She can't hear or speak so why would they waste time teaching her? Besides, they were too busy investing in Saul's future."

"Every Hebrew child has the right to the knowledge of our people." Jude set his back straight. "I know girls only get a few years but those are precious times." His gaze fell soft on Arava. "I can't imagine being denied that gift." The weight of his gifting of knowledge and its recent expansion wrapped around him both like a comforting blanket and a heavy responsibility.

"I don't know how much she understands." Salome gestured back to Arava. "She only practices letters. I don't think she understands how to form them into words or what they mean."

Arava's head dipped low again and she hid her hands behind her back.

"She thinks she's in trouble." Salome shot a helpless gaze at Jude. "She's afraid we're angry with her for scribing when she's been banned from doing so by her father."

Jude's soul blazed with a mixture of anger and compassion. "Salome, show me your gesture for 'writing'."

She held up one hand and took the first finger of her other and made motions over her palm. "Like a scribe with a quill and scroll."

Jude copied the movement. "And 'teach'. How do you say 'teach'?"

Salome put her hand to her head and pushed out toward her brother.

After watching carefully, Jude repeated the motion until he got it right. He stepped to place himself directly in front of Arava. Fighting every urge within himself to reach out and lift her chin, he tucked his head so his eyes could meet hers. There, he patiently waited until she lifted her face.

With slow movements, he held up his palm to her and opened and closed his hand. "Come." He pointed to himself. "I." He moved his hand to his head and pushed it toward her. "Teach." He held out his palm to her. "Arava." Turning his hand over, he motioned marks into his hand with his other finger. "Write."

Her eyes grew large as she shook her head.

He nodded, trying to sway her.

Tears formed in her eyes as she continued to violently shake her head.

He gently reached for her hand.

She pulled away at his touch.

He tried again; this time moving even slower. He took her hand in his and bent toward the sand. With slow, deliberate movements, he drew a symbol in the dirt with her finger before letting go of her hand. "Alpha." He pointed to the letter and looked up into her eyes. Emphasizing the word with his lips near her face, he repeated, "Alpha."

She glanced down at the letter as a smile tugged at her lips.

"That's where we will begin."

CHAPTER 30

For the rest of the week, Jude spent his time sitting in the sand beside his family's booth showing Arava how to properly write each letter of their people's tongue. It was a slow process as he was ever mindful of the line between not pushing her frustrations and keeping her challenged.

As the rest of the family disassembled their temporary dwelling, Jude soaked in the freedom of being able to get one more lesson in before they went back to the villa.

With as clean strokes as he could manage in the sand, he scribed a few letters together.

Arava looked up at him with confusion clear on her face.

He chuckled. "I know they're not in order. This," he pointed to the ground, "is your name." He pushed an open palm toward her. "Arava."

She looked down at the letters and back at him.

"Arava." He pushed his palm to her again. "Arava."

Her gaze dropped to the dirt.

Jude studied her as she studied the letters. Dark strands of hair slipped from under her headwrap as she bent to deeply consider his scribe. He wanted earnestly to tuck them back behind her ear but knew he had no right. Instead, he watched her brow furrow over her eyes as she intently stared at the marks.

Slowly, she lifted a hand and pointed to herself.

"Yes." Jude shook his head for reassurance. "Arava."

With shaking fingertips, she traced his letters over and over again, making deeper imprints in the sand. When she was satisfied, she looked up at him and motioned.

He watched her hands come up to her chin as she wiggled her fingers inward and moved her hands away from her face. "I don't understand."

She grunted and looked around.

Salome happened to be passing by with a basket full of branches.

"Salome," Jude called to her, "Arava is trying to tell me something."

The younger sister came close and watched Arava's movements. "Oh."

Jude noticed his sister's cheeks bloom pink. "What?"

"That's her sign for…" she put her fingers over her lips attempting to hold back a laugh, "…for you."

He flicked his gaze to Arava as she repeated the sign. "What's she doing?"

"'Scroll beard.'" Salome let out a laugh. "See her

fingers wiggling like she's unrolling a scroll. But she combines the movement with a downward motion away from her chin like a long beard. Together, 'scroll beard.' It's her sign for 'Jude.'"

He pointed to himself. "Jude?"

Arava nodded deeply.

He glanced down at the sand. "Oh," with his finger, he spelled out his name, "Jude."

With determined motions, Arava followed his letters with her finger, creating deeper wells in the sand. After a few times, she lifted her palm and pushed it toward him.

A warm sensation filled Jude's soul. "Yes." He nodded vigorously. "Jude."

She settled back on her heels as she stared down at both names.

Jude studied the two words together as well. A profound longing grew inside him. Something he'd denied until that moment. "I think that's enough for now." He rose and dusted sand from his tunic. "Salome, Arava is free to help you return the supplies to the villa."

"Where are you going?"

"I need to speak with James about something." He headed to search for his brother.

James and Joseph were hard at work breaking down the last wall of the booth.

"Ahh," James called upon his approach, "finished

your lesson for the day?"

"Yes." Jude grabbed a pole to help. "Arava has made great progress, and I wanted to speak with you about something."

Unraveling a knot, James hummed. "Well, go on then. Speak what's on your mind."

"Oh," Jude flicked a glance at Joseph, "right now?"

James set the freed pole down. "Unless it can wait."

Jude glanced over his shoulder at Arava who was holding an empty basket that Salome was filling with the foliage they'd hung to decorate the booth.

"Speak, brother," Joseph encouraged.

Jude turned back to both of them. "I'd like to wed Arava."

Joseph dropped the pole in his hand nearly striking James' foot.

"Careful." James' foot came up with the near miss.

"Forgive me." Joseph picked up the wayward beam.

"Now," James turned his attention back to Jude, "where is this coming from?"

"I know I've set my intentions on other women before but Adonai has seen to block me from joining with those others." Jude put a hand on the back of his neck. "Spending time with Arava this week…I don't know…." He let his hand drop. "I believe she may be the woman Adonai has designed for me."

"So, you wish to enter a betrothal agreement with

her?"

He lowered his head before his oldest brother. "I was hoping we could skip that process."

"And what?" James held up his hands. "Go straight to a wedding feast?"

"I know it's against tradition." Jude lifted a shoulder. "But we hold onto that tradition so a man has time to prepare a place for the bride. A place has already been prepared for our family in the villa."

James glanced toward his sisters and Arava. "That seems to be true."

"So why wait for months or years?" Jude threw up his hands. "If she agrees to the arrangement, I'd like to make her part of our family as soon as possible. Give her a proper place among us."

"Oh, I'm sure Salome will have no problem with that," Joseph teased. "And Ima already loves her like a daughter."

James flicked his gaze to his brother. "That's certainly true, too."

"Besides," Jude added, "Arava has been more than helpful. She's very willing to learn and to work."

James pinched his chin. "Willing hands are always welcome." He set his gaze on Jude. "What are we going to do about her dowry?"

"I don't care about such things."

"She might." James waved to Arava. "What will she have to care for herself if something happens to you?"

"She'll have you." Jude pointed to James. "And Joseph, and Salome, and even Lydia and Ima. She'll have a family. That's a lot more than what she has right now."

James was quiet for several moments.

"Brother," Jude stepped closer, "everyone in her life has either tried to hide her away or fix her." He hung his head. "Even me. I was trying to fix her as if she was broken. After much prayer and consideration, I think Adonai leaves some unhealed whom He knows are not broken." He lifted his eyes to Arava. "She follows Adonai regardless of the function of her ears or tongue." He turned back to James. "I believe her soul is exactly where it belongs; in the hands of Adonai."

As James quietly considered Jude's words, a darkness clouded his features. "If you do this, you'll seal your fate with the council. They will never allow you a seat among them with a wife that's...like Arava."

Jude had not allowed that reality to sink into his thoughts. The most respected and knowledgeable men in all Israel sat among the Council. He was closer than ever at the chance for a place in their ranks. If he took Arava as his life partner, he'd be relinquishing that dream...forever. "My fate is already sealed by my brother. I choose Arava."

"Well," James fought back a smirk as he put a hand on his Jude's shoulder, "I guess Chislon and Talia were right."

Jude flinched at the mention of Arava's family members who, in his mind, had entirely abandoned her.

"Arava is where she is supposed to be...with us."

Jude wrapped his brother in his arms. "Thank you."

"Don't thank me yet." James chuckled in his hold. "You've got to figure out a way to present the arrangement to her." He pulled back from the embrace. "Seeing as how we can't talk to her father about it."

"Leave it with me," Jude promised. "I will get Salome to help me learn more of her gestures so I can speak with her properly. I'd like her to have a voice in this decision."

"As it should be," James agreed. "Now, help us get the rest of these poles down."

CHAPTER 31

Two months later, on the eve of the Feast of Dedication, Jude stood on nervous toes in the courtyard of the villa.

He'd spent weeks learning the exact signs from Salome to ask Arava to be his wife. His sister, being more than willing to make her connection with Arava permanent, practiced his question with him every day.

With a wide smile, Arava had agreed to the arrangement and been ushered away by the females of the house to prepare for her wedding feast.

When the time arrived, guests had been carefully called and the villa was filled with food and musicians. Remembering the shofar, Jude specifically requested instruments that would make bold sounds so Arava could feel their vibrations during the celebration.

As he stood patiently waiting, Jude considered the feast ahead. Not only would those present be celebrating his union but also the remembrance of Adonai's faithfulness. The Feast of the Maccabees, as it was often called, was a time to reflect on Adonai's provisions.

After the Temple had been desecrated by the

Syrians under Antiochus Epiphanes, Adonai revealed himself by keeping the oil of a single day's measure burning for eight days for Judas Maccabaeus. When the Temple was finally cleansed, the Hebrews commemorated the time with a yearly week-long feast. During the week, lamps are lit in homes, synagogues, and the Temple to remind people of the light Adonai kept burning. The feast calls for joy and merriment, and no public mourning is permitted.

Jude's chest puffed with the joy that filled his soul. He wouldn't have to worry about mourning this week. Soon, his bride, the one Adonai had provided, would be ready, and he would spend the week in pure merriment with her by his side.

When he could wait no longer, he ascended the steps two at a time. In the upper room, Arava stood among his sisters, mother, sister-in-law, and the female servants. Jude's chest burned as if it were going to expand through his skin.

The woman who stood before him was more ravishing than any he'd ever seen. She was washed and wrapped in a dress that perfectly fit her. Her skin was bright and the scent of oils and herbs perfumed off her. He was utterly intoxicated and care fled him like a bird when the rains ceased.

He held up his palm and opened and closed his fingers.

With fluid grace, Arava made her way to him.

The two carefully descended the steps, followed by the women, to where the men and the rest of the guests awaited them in the open courtyard.

"I know you can't hear me," Jude whispered beside Arava's ear. "But I love you, Arava. And as long as Adonai grants me breath, I will love you."

Ethan stood with James and Joseph on either side of him in the open area.

Jude led Arava toward the three. His Rabbi had graciously agreed to step in as a representative of Arava's family as they had made it clear that she was no longer counted among them.

Once they stood in front of the men, Jude lifted the sheer veil to confirm that Arava lay underneath.

Her bright smile shone back at him as her cheeks bloomed a bright pink.

He lowered her veil back into place and faced Ethan. "I ask for this woman to be my wife," he let his voice ring out as boldly as he could. "She is my wife, and I am her husband from this day and forever."

Ethan reached for Arava's hand and placed it in Jude's. "She is yours."

Shouts rang out around them as the music started and filled the air with vibrations.

Salome was the first to kiss their cheeks, followed swiftly by Mary and Elissa.

Jude and Arava were passed from person to person receiving blessings and words of praise.

With a melancholy heart, Jude took in each one, knowing his wife could not hear them for herself.

For the rest of the night, Jude kept Arava's hand in his. He feared releasing her would bring his wonderful dream to an end. Only when Salome requested the bride to join the women for a dance did he finally loosen his grip.

"I promise to return her," Salome called over her shoulder as she led Arava toward the musicians.

Coming out of his merriment daze, he noticed James and Peter in what appeared to be a heated conversation. Not wanting one moment of his wedding feast to be ruined, he made his way toward them. "Something I can help with?"

Peter kept a fierce gaze on James and closed his mouth as if Jude had interrupted him mid-statement.

"Nothing you need to be concerned with brother." James assured him with a hand on his shoulder.

Jude gave a warning glance to Peter. "I will enjoy my wedding feast much more if we can settle whatever debate removes my brother from enjoying it as well."

"We were merely discussing a concern that has come up among the widows." Peter waved him off.

"It seems to have grown into a great concern," James argued.

Jude grew frustrated with their hedged words. "What's the problem?"

James sighed. "It seems that as the colder weather

has descended upon us, some of the Hellenistic widows believe we are favoring the more Hebrew widows over them."

"That's absurd." Jude flung his hand toward Peter.

The fisherman lifted defending palms. "There have been many complaints that some are being neglected in the daily distributions."

"We make sure the rations are spread as much as we can," Jude explained. "Some days there is simply not enough to go around. We are only so many with so much."

"I understand. The twelve of us disciples have been forced to spend less time teaching to make the increasing visits." Peter lifted a shoulder. "Even with that sacrifice, the complaints grow. We must do something to resolve this."

"Jesus might have selected you twelve for himself as students," James maintained, "but that doesn't mean there weren't more who followed him. I think we should consult them on this matter."

Jude turned to his brother. "Can this at least wait until after the feast?"

"I think it's a fair request." James flicked a glance at Peter. "As soon as this week is complete, we will call a meeting among all the followers and sort this out."

True to their word, James and Peter held their peace until Jude's wedding feast ended. The morning of the following day brought bitter cold and a villa full of Way Followers.

Peter stood on the steps to address the gathering. "We've heard the complaints among the widows," his voice bounced off the stone walls. "It is not right that we should give up preaching the word of Adonai to serve tables. Therefore, pick out from among yourselves seven men of good reputation, full of the Spirit and of wisdom, whom we will appoint to this duty. But we will devote ourselves to prayer and the ministry of the word."

Jude listened to agreement musings wash through the group.

Names and men were pressed forward until seven stood in front of the rest.

Peter looked at each man. "Philip. Prochoru. Nicanor. Timon. Parmenas. Nicolaus. And Stephen. You have been chosen." He waved toward the disciples. "Come."

The men who followed Jesus laid hands on the seven while Peter prayed over them. Afterward, Peter dismissed the other Way Followers and took the seven men to the upper room with the other disciples to share with them where they would be serving among the city and supply them provisions for their first visits.

Jude took the opportunity to steal away to the kitchen where he found Arava helping the women prepare for the day.

He slid his hands around her waist and pulled her

close. With gentleness, he kissed her forehead and laid his cheek there.

Without words, she squeezed him back and pressed into his embrace.

Jude knew there was a room full of men waiting for him to go out into the city to teach about Jesus. There were widows to be fed but now their charge would be in the hands of seven men Adonai had prepared. His burden felt lifted and yet shifted at the same time. He was free from visiting widows but his continued lessons with Arava only flamed his passion for teaching. She might be his only student but she was his favorite.

He inhaled her scent which still smelled of bridal oils. At that moment, he wanted nothing more than to hold onto his wife. He wanted to stay with her more than the draw of an ark full of scrolls or eager people with hearts open to hear of Jesus.

With reluctance, he held her out to look into her eyes. He knew he'd have the rest of his life to hold her and, still, he didn't want to let go.

He put up his palm and pushed it toward her. "Arava." Turning it around, he pointed to himself. "Jude." Then he pressed both his hands together.

She nodded rapidly and wrapped herself against him.

He knew she understood his promise to keep her.

What's Next?

Which will conquer, forgiveness or revenge?

Lydia wanted to flee her cramped family home to seek new paths in the wide world, but tradition and family expectations kept her shackled to her position.

When her oldest brother's radical teachings and unbelievable miracles convinced her that Jesus was Messiah, Lydia traded her life of serving herself for one of serving others.

While helping new converts in Jerusalem, she fell in love with another servant. A man named Stephen quickly won her heart and her hand with his bright eyes and humble spirit.

Before their vows could be completed, local Pharisees murdered her betrothed. Claiming their religious right to justice, they escaped charges of his death. His innocent blood marked their already-stained hands. With her partner in life and service stolen from her, Lydia is left wondering what path to follow.

Will she hold to the Way and what her brother taught about forgiveness or will she turn away from everything to seek justice for her beloved?

Experience the spark that fanned the flames of change in this engaging Biblical fiction story, *Lydia*, book 5 of the Servant Siblings series.

More from Jenifer Jennings:

Special Collections and Boxed Sets

Biblical Historical stories from the Old Testament to the New, these special boxed editions offer a great way to catch up or to fall in love with Jenifer Jennings' books for the first time.

Faith Finder Series: Books 1-3
Faith Finders Series: Books 4-6
The Rebekah Series: Books 1-3
Servant Siblings Series: Books 1-3

* * *

Faith Finders Series:

Go deeper into the stories of these familiar faith heroines.

Midwives of Moses
Wilderness Wanderer
Crimson Cord
A Stolen Wife
At His Feet
Lasting Legacy

* * *

The Rebekah Series:

Follow Rebekah on her faith journey through life.

The Stranger
The Journey
The Hope

* * *

Servant Siblings Series:

*They were Jesus' siblings,
but they become His followers.*

James
Joseph
Assia
Jude
Lydia
Simon
Salome

* * *

Paul's Patrons Series:

*Little known supporters of Paul's ministry have their
own stories to tell.*

Raging Sea
Warring Church

**Find these titles at your favorite retailer or at:
jeniferjennings.com/books**

About the Author

Jenifer Jennings writes Historical novels that immerse readers in ancient worlds filled with Biblical characters and faith-building stories. Coming to faith in Jesus at seventeen, she spends her days falling in love with her Savior through the study of His Word. Jenifer has a Bachelor's in Women's Ministry and graduated with distinction while earning her Master's in Biblical Languages. When she's not working on her latest book, Jenifer can be found on a date with her hardworking husband or mothering their two children.

If you'd like to keep up with new releases, receive spiritual encouragement, and get your hands on a FREE book, then join Jenifer's Newsletter at:
jeniferjennings.com/gift

Made in the USA
Middletown, DE
02 March 2024